MIDNIGHT IS MY TIME

4/28/2019
R. X S.

MIDNIGHT IS MY TIME

By

MIKE DELLOSSO

For the loves of my life:
Jen, Laura, Abby, Caroline, Elizabeth, and Nora

Acknowledgments

First, I'd like to thank my God for giving me the opportunity to write books. It is a blessing and responsibility I don't take lightly.

I'd like to give thanks to my wife and daughters who inspire me and encourage me. They make every day worth waking up to.

Big thanks must go to my editors, Darla Crass and Denise Loock, special ladies who do a marvelous job of polishing and buffing and making a story even better.

Thanks to Eddie and Lighthouse Publishing of the Carolinas for having such an amazing vision. The heart that beats within this publishing house is what drew me to them.

And lastly, where would I be without my readers? Thank you, thank you, thank you for supporting me over this past decade of writing books. You keep me going. Really.

Chapter 1

The diner was nothing special, nothing to take note of, nothing to remember beyond this moment. One in probably a couple thousand just like it hidden in small towns across the barren landscape. To the locals, it was a reprieve from a day's worth of toil and a chance to connect and catch up on gossip and news. And to the occasional journeyman looking for an inexpensive meal and place to rest his road-weary legs, it was an oasis.

And Andy Mayer needed an oasis.

He glanced around the place from his booth by the door. He didn't even know where he was, but it was definitely a mining town. Weren't most of them nowadays? Somewhere in central Pennsylvania, he supposed. It all looked the same since The Event. Dirt, rocks, dust, and a few anemic trees clinging to life, stretching their scrawny branches skyward like captives begging for food.

Andy removed his Stetson and sat it on the seat next to him. Already the locals were staring. It was one thing to be a stranger, a whole different animal being a freak too.

To his left was the counter, topped with polished Formica and lined with vinyl-upholstered stools. Behind that, the sounds and smells of a busy kitchen. Pots rattled and clanged; the grill sizzled and spit. Two booths away, a red-haired kid with a dirty face and buckteeth watched Andy with wide eyes. His mother ordered him to turn around. Didn't he know it wasn't polite to stare? She gave Andy a sheepish smile of apology and averted her eyes.

Finally, the waitress came and set a menu in front of him.

"Here ya go, sugar. Anything to drink?"

He didn't miss the hesitation in her voice and the pity in her eyes when she looked him in the face. Or was it disgust? Hard to tell the difference. She was a busty woman, middle-aged with big hair, long lashes. Her nametag said "Cindy."

Andy had noticed the drill outside behind the diner. The joint had fresh water from a real subterranean spring. Not many did anymore. "Big glass of your water, please," he said. He lowered his head so she didn't have to look at him.

"Wonderful. I'll give ya a couple minutes to look that menu over and be right back." She turned and walked away, her wide hips swinging side to side like a grandfather clock's pendulum.

Andy opened the menu and studied the options. If the smell of the kitchen already had his stomach rumbling, the description of the meals in the menu tied it in knots. The fried chicken platter looked good. He'd get extra biscuits.

Cindy returned with a tall glass of clear water and placed it in front of him. "There ya go. Where ya from?"

Andy stared at the glass. It'd been weeks since he'd seen water that clear. "Kentucky."

She glanced at the Stetson on the seat next to him. "You a cowboy?"

"Was one." Five years ago, Andy Mayer had stumbled upon the Circle K ranch in southern Kentucky. It was a good place to bury himself, to avoid the prying eyes of society, and to get lost in the land of horses. But as it always did, trouble found him, this time in the form of Dean Shannon. A week ago, Andy stuffed a duffel bag with clothes and left, started walking northeast. He had no idea why it was north and east other than the fact that he felt pulled there like metal to a magnet. At first, he'd tried to resist, tried for three days. He'd always wanted to go west, and in fact had set out toward St. Louis, but each day the pull had grown stronger until eventually he could no longer defy it. He had to obey, follow the path of least resistance. He didn't know where he was headed, didn't know when he'd reach his destination; he only knew he had to keep moving, had to head northeast.

"Sounds like there's a story there."

He shrugged. "Not much of one."

"Where ya headed?"

"Northeast."

She paused, removed a steno pad from her apron pocket, and slipped a pen from above her ear. "Not much for talkin', huh?"

"Don't have much to say, ma'am."

"Just like a cowboy."

When Andy didn't say anything, Cindy clicked the pen. "Well, what can I get ya?"

"Fried chicken platter, extra biscuits, please."

While she jotted his order on the pad, she said, "You picked a good one, cowboy. Our fried chicken is the best in the county."

Behind Andy, the diner's door opened and the bells chimed.

"It'll only be a few minutes." Cindy winked at him and disappeared behind a group of three men who'd entered. They were all dressed in dirty jeans and sweat-stained T-shirts. Looked like they'd been working the mines all day. They stopped in front of Andy's booth. The one in front rapped his large knuckles against the tabletop.

"Hey, cowboy."

Andy looked up. They were young—mid to late twenties— and big. Miners for sure. Full of muscle and attitude. He knew the type; they grew 'em big in Kentucky too.

One of the two in the back snickered and whispered something to the other about the "freak."

The one in front, the largest of the three, drilled Andy with beady green eyes. He wore a faded John Deere hat and had a spotty day's worth of growth on his face. "You're in our booth, cowboy."

Andy said nothing but broke eye contact. These guys were looking for trouble, and he wanted no part of it. He wanted to eat and then to move on in peace. Head northeast. To a destination he knew nothing of.

The big guy rapped again on the tabletop like he was some persistent salesman unwilling to leave any door unanswered. "You deaf, cowboy? I said you're in our booth."

A hush fell over the diner and heads turned. The evening's entertainment had arrived. The kid with the red hair and beaver teeth was staring again. Andy met his eyes and found in them an innocence only children possessed. The boy couldn't have been more than four years old.

Andy interlaced his fingers on the tabletop. He stared at the kid, hoping some of that innocence would permeate the rest of the diner and the three punks looking for trouble would leave.

It didn't happen. John Deere bent at the waist and leaned in close to Andy as if he were speaking to a toddler. "You gonna move, freak, or are we gonna have to move you? Find another booth. This here one is ours. Always is." His breath smelled like tobacco.

Still, Andy said nothing. He looked one more time at the kid, gave a little smile, then scooted out of the booth. He wasn't there for a fight, just some food.

"That's it, cowboy." John Deere reached for Andy's Stetson and crumpled it in his massive hand. "Oh, wait, you forgot your hat." He handed it to Andy. "Can't be a real cowboy without your hat, right?"

The other two laughed and elbowed each other.

Cindy approached and pushed her way through the miners. "Jason, knock it off. Cowboy, you sit yourself right back down. You were here first. It's your booth. These three kids can find another one."

Andy didn't move, didn't make eye contact either. He held his Stetson in both hands and worked the wrinkles out of it. His mother had given it to him years ago. Just a day before she died. A day before Andy stood by and watched the life slip out of her. The red-haired kid still watched, eyes wide.

"C'mon, Cindy." Jason's voice rose. "We're here every night, pay your lousy salary, and you're gonna side with the freak?"

"Back off, boys." Cindy turned to Andy. "Cowboy, c'mon. Sit yourself down here."

Andy made a move for the booth, but Jason was having none of it. He wasn't the type to be humiliated by a woman and a freak, especially not in public. He stepped past Cindy, nearly knocking her over, and put a hand on Andy's chest. There was hate and hurtin' in his eyes. He was hungry for more than dinner. Violence was what he craved.

Andy glanced at the man's hand on his chest. The creases of his knuckles and the rims of his nails were caked with dirt. Mining dust stained his leathery skin. Andy then raised his eyes so he met the punk's glare. A hint of something hid in Jason's small eyes. Not fear. No, he was too arrogant and dumb to fear. It was uncertainty. He was used to bullying his way around but not used to bullying freaks. Andy unnerved him.

"Jason, let it go," Cindy said. Behind Jason, an elderly couple slid out of their booth and headed for the door without paying. They'd probably seen this sideshow before and wanted no part of it.

Andy took a step back, creating space between his chest and Jason's hand.

Cindy grabbed Jason by the arm and tried to pull him out of the way. "You boys get outta here, you hear me? You're not welcome here no more."

Anger flashed in Jason's eyes, and the muscles along his jawline flexed. He spun and shoved Cindy, sending her clattering into the booth and spilling the sugar across the tabletop.

Andy hoped the redhead wasn't watching. He didn't want the kid to see what was to come next.

In a motion so quick and smooth that it even caught him by surprise, Andy snatched Jason by the wrist and twisted his arm behind his back. He ran the big guy forward until his waist met the counter, then slammed his head down hard. Jason came up with glassy eyes and a nose spouting blood. The other two cursed and jumped in, swinging thick arms like windmills. A familiar darkness moved over Andy, a deep shadow of something fierce and malevolent, something not of this world. It came from inside him, from some deep cavern within his calloused soul. It emerged, ugly and twisted, and demanded control. It was the master now, and Andy its helpless servant.

The rest was a smudge in his mind.

He caught moments, like movie stills, flashing by, images from a dream, really, blurred and disconnected. His elbow connecting with a face, an abdomen. The sound of teeth breaking. Grunts, groans. Cursing. His foot slamming into a jeaned knee. Glass breaking. Sweat, blood. The crack and pop of breaking bones. Everything beyond his immediate reach faded out of view. Cindy, the kid—*God, the kid*—the other patrons, they vanished into a dark fog.

Then there was nothing. He stood, heaving, fists clenched, sweat dripping from his nose. The darkness was gone now, vanished as quickly as it had arrived to hijack his humanity and turn him into something . . . nonhuman. The three miners—the punks—lay on the floor, Jason motionless, the other two writhing like eels out of water. The big one held his forearm and gritted his teeth. It was cocked at a sickening angle, unnatural. The other held his knee and bawled like a toddler.

Andy looked up, found Cindy, found the kid. The innocence was gone, replaced by fear. Cindy's eyes were large. Her mouth moved as if she wanted to say something, but nothing came out. The kid's mouth hung open like the hinges had busted. His mother grabbed his arm and hurried him out the door.

From somewhere behind the counter, Andy heard the words, "Somebody call the cops." Then he was gone, out the door, into the blazing evening sun, and across the parking lot. His feet slapped the asphalt and matched the tempo of his heart thumping in his throat. He hit the road running full speed and kept at it until his legs and lungs could carry him no farther. There, somewhere miles down another road he had stumbled upon after crossing a clearing and picking his way through a small but thick patch of woods, he spotted a four-foot corrugated drainage pipe that crossed under the road and emptied into a ditch. He crawled inside, pulled his knees to his chest, tilted his hat forward, and let the tears come.

That wasn't him back there. He wasn't a man prone to violence. He didn't want a fight. But he had fought; it had happened again. Just like with Dean. The darkness had swept in and filtered through every molecule of his being, taking control, lusting for violence and blood and havoc. It had once again done irreparable damage.

And though the drainage pipe was cramped and hard, it didn't take him long to fall asleep where he was met by images of devils and monsters. Gruesome beasts performing grisly acts of violence and perversion.

He awoke with a start. Beyond the pipe, the sky was dark, the stars visible. The air had a chill to it. He'd had the same nightmare the past three nights. It was part of the pull, the strange force tugging him northeast, always northeast.

Chapter 2

Her world was dark, a black canvas that stretched to infinity in every direction. But that didn't keep her from seeing. Since she was eight years old, she'd seen the world, not through optic nerves transmitting impulses to the brain but through her other senses. Her ability to take information collected from her auditory and olfactory nerves and thousands of receptors in her flesh enabled her to form images in her mind. Those images evolved out of her distant memory of colors, light, and shapes, then morphed into ghostly stills that shimmered and blinked like dreams from another dimension. This was how she saw the world.

And she saw him there, in the drainage pipe. As she made her way down the barren road, alone, being careful not to scuff her feet, she heard his even, steady breathing—sleep breathing. She smelled the aroma of frying oil and horses and sweat and fear. Anger was there too. Lots of anger.

Carefully, she made her way down the embankment, picking her way along, using her white cane to sense—to see—the changes in terrain, the rocks, the stunted shrubbery, the patches of dried grass. Finally, she made it to the bottom of the culvert that ran parallel to the road. Standing there, listening, she saw him against the black backdrop of her mind. He was a large man; she could tell by the depth of his breathing. And he was alone, his breathing solitary and lonesome. Obviously, he did not belong in a drainage pipe, which meant he had a story and, no doubt, one rife with heartache and hurt and violence. She had a mind to leave him. His story was none of her business. His drainage pipe slumber was not her concern.

But it was. She felt it. This man had a story, yes, and it was time for his story to intersect with her story. A union of tragedies. Over the years, the sensing of her heart had grown as heightened as her other, more physical senses.

She would wake him gently. He was not the type of man who startled easily, but when he did, it came with thrashing arms and swinging fists. She had experience with such men.

The girl approached the drainage pipe with caution as if she were approaching a sleeping lion. She could tell by the way the man's breaths reverberated against the corrugated metal that he had inserted himself at least four feet into the pipe. Her white cane was five feet long.

One hand against the pipe's opening, she inserted the cane and held it in the air like a probe moving through a catheter. She pushed it forward until it found its mark and nudged the sleeping man. Suddenly, quicker than she could react, a hand snatched the cane and yanked it away from her. She tripped on the lip of the opening, dropped her backpack, and tumbled forward into the pipe. Two hands, as firm and strong as iron, gripped her shoulders, lifted her, and slammed her against the unforgiving metal. Air escaped her lungs in a short burst.

"Who are you? Where did you come from?"

His voice was rough, gravelly, his words slightly slurred. She had aroused him from a deep sleep; he was disoriented and frightened.

"Missy. My name's Missy."

He held her there, pressing her against the pipe, breathing hard. His breath smelled like stale coffee and his body like sweat and dirt. She heard his heart thumping hard and quick in his chest. The soft scratch of fabric and the shift of his weight indicated he turned his head back and forth.

"How did you find me? Did anyone follow you?"

"Can you let go of me first?" Oddly, Missy felt no fear in the presence of this man. Normally, confronting a strange man who had found refuge in a drainage pipe would instill a certain amount of panic in anyone. But fear had no place here. Not for her. Not with him. It was as if she had known him a long time ago, had trusted him, and even befriended him, only to just now be reunited.

Slowly, he softened his grip until his hands released her. He exhaled.

"Are you alone?"

"Boy, that's a loaded question. Yes. I was walking along the road and heard you breathing."

There was a short pause and silence until her white cane clinked against the metal of the pipe. He did not hand it to her immediately. "You're blind."

"No, I'm Missy. And you are?"

"You can't see." He sounded relieved to make such a discovery.

"I see, just not like you do. I probably see more than you do."

He placed the cane's grip in her hand.

"Proper introductions haven't been made until both parties share their name," Missy said.

More silence. The man drew in a long, deep breath. He scratched his rough face. She assumed he was weighing the risk of giving his name to a total stranger who had found him hiding in a pipe.

"How do I know you're not with them?"

"With who? The police? FBI?"

He said nothing.

"Since when did the FBI send blind agents on foot patrol in the middle of nowhere?"

"Where did you come from?"

"Pittsburgh."

"You walked all this way?"

She shrugged. "And hitched it some."

"Why? Who are you running from?"

He was perceptive too.

She felt no need to lie to him. They were meant to meet; they were meant to join paths and travel together. Companions. Call it fate or providence or anything else, but Missy knew it was meant to be. "My stepfather."

"Mean guy?"

"You have no idea."

"I bet I do."

A few beats of awkward silence passed between them before he said, "Andy."

"Andy. That's a nice name. Simple. Honest. Innocent."

"Believe me. There's nothing innocent about me." And with that, he maneuvered his way around Missy and out of the drainage pipe.

He walked away, his shoes shuffling through the dirt.

Missy found her backpack, swung it onto her shoulder, and scrambled out of the pipe as well. "Wait. You can't just leave."

He stopped. Turned. "Why not?"

"You're going to leave me standing here? Alone?"

"You made it this far. From Pittsburgh."

"I'm blind."

"But you see better than I do. You said so yourself."

"I need to come with you."

"You don't want to do that."

"Yes. I do. I need to."

He paused and made no sound. In the distance, a hawk screeched, and beyond that, she heard the deep rumble of a pickup with a modified exhaust barreling down the road. Maybe a half mile away.

"A truck's coming," she said. "We could hitch a ride."

"Not gonna happen."

"How are you gonna stop me?"

"Really? You're blind. I'm bigger than you. Quite a bit bigger."

Missy approached him. Her cane tapped the ground in front of her until it touched his shoe. She lifted her head.

"I'm coming."

"Look." He sighed. "Trouble follows me, okay? Always has. I don't want you to have any part of that."

The truck grew closer, louder. She ascended the embankment using her cane as a climbing tool. "But we're going to the same place." Her foot slipped, and she expected him to steady her, but he didn't.

"What do you mean?"

When they reached the top, she was breathless, and the truck was nearly upon them. She waved her stick to get the driver's attention and lifted her thumb.

She heard Andy climbing the embankment, his shoes slipping on the loose soil. He stood beside her. He, too, breathed heavily. "What do you mean we're going to the same place?"

The truck's engine rumbled loudly as it slowed.

"We might as well stick together since we're both headed north."

"Where north? And how did you know I was headed north?"

She just knew. She felt it. They were to be companions.

The truck stopped. The door opened and the driver, a young guy, said, "Hop in."

Missy put one hand on the truck's door and said to Andy, "Well? Are you coming?"

Andy raised his voice over the growl of the engine. "How did you know I was headed north?"

"Maine," she said. "You're going to Maine. So am I. Now can you please open the door for me?"

Andy brushed past her and opened the door.

Chapter 3

The truck driver's name was Colin. Mid-twenties and bulky, he hadn't shaved for several days. A faded, tattered ball cap perched atop his head. He reminded Andy of the miners back at the diner. Jason and his two stooges.

Colin didn't say much.

Missy did most of the talking. She sat next to Colin and chatted him up about the unchanging weather, the flat terrain, her worn sneakers, and a mutt named Lucky she'd had when she was seven.

Colin barely acknowledged Missy's presence but kept glancing at Andy. Andy tipped his Stetson lower on his forehead and tried to ignore his host's fascination. Something about Colin didn't feel right, didn't sit right with him. The guy was odd—too quiet, too tense. Then again, he'd picked up a blind girl and her pet freak. Anyone would be uneasy with that duo sitting next to him.

But more than that, something about him, about the way his eyes shifted from one mirror to another, the rigid posture of his body in the seat, the way he gripped the steering wheel—it was all unnatural.

Missy didn't see it, of course, but Andy wondered if she could sense it, hear it in the guy's occasional grunts and one-word answers. He wondered if she could feel a negative vibe emanating from him like compressed air waves from a subwoofer.

Suddenly, Colin's foot grew heavier on the accelerator, and the truck growled and lunged forward. Missy stopped talking and leaned into Andy.

"What's going on?" Andy said. He didn't trust Colin at all.

Colin massaged the steering wheel and dipped his chin. "There's a diner up ahead. Merlin's. I'm dropping you two off there."

Missy stared blankly out of the windshield. "You can't take us any farther?"

"Nope."

"But we've only been driving for a little while."

"I can take you back where I found you," Colin said.

Missy's eyes darted left to right in nervous fashion as she reached for Andy's hand.

The truck's engine coughed as Colin worked the gear stick, and it accelerated even more.

Over a gentle rise, the diner appeared on the left. It sat alone in the middle of a clearing surrounded by a crumbling parking lot and a few struggling, wiry shrubs in need of trimming. Two pickups waited in the lot, one around the side of the building, the other near the front entrance. Both were weatherworn and rusted around the corners. Across the road sprawled a barren field, nothing but clumpy, dry dirt and a few isolated patches of brown grass barely ankle-high. The wasteland spread all the way to the horizon before yielding to a thin line of leafless trees. Beyond the horizon, a storm loomed, its leading edge as dark as oil. Behind it, the sky roiled like an angry upside-down ocean. But the clouds would dump no rain, at least not any amount that would mean anything. It hadn't rained enough to soak the ground in well near ten years.

Andy didn't like this diner. He rarely had a good experience in these types of places. And he didn't want to drag Missy into any of his problems. "How 'bout you just drop me off and take the girl to the next town," he said, hoping Colin's sudden interest in getting rid of them was due mostly to the fact that he had a two-hundred-and-twenty-pound freak in the cab of his truck.

Colin slowed the truck and steered it into the parking lot right up to the door of the diner. "This is it," he said, looking straight ahead. "For both of you."

Missy turned her face toward Andy. "Looks like this is it, big guy."

Andy exited the truck and helped Missy down from the cab. The truck roared, tires spun in the loose soil, and black smoke billowed from the exhaust as it tore out of the lot, leaving a rooster tail of dust in its wake. Colin had brought them this far, but compared to the trek that lay ahead of them, this leg of the trip had been a mere hop.

The interior of the diner matched the exterior. This was an establishment on life support. If it had ever seen better days, they were a distant memory. Only one booth was occupied. An elderly man with rough skin, wiry gray hair, and glassy eyes fed himself scrambled eggs and toast. He barely noticed when Andy and Missy entered.

They seated themselves in a booth by the window and were soon greeted by the waitress—a young woman, thin, sunken cheeks, and hollow eyes. She glanced at Missy, then at Andy. He could tell by the way her lips parted and eyes widened that he had frightened her. She dropped her gaze to the table.

"Get you something to drink?"

"Just water for me," Missy said.

"It's recycled. That okay? We ain't got no pump here."

"That's fine."

Andy did not look at the waitress. "Coffee, please."

They both ordered the breakfast special of two eggs, home fries, and two pieces of toast. When the food arrived, Missy said, "So what's your story?"

Andy removed his Stetson and sat it beside him in the booth. He then put a forkful of eggs in his mouth and chewed slowly. The food was surprisingly good. Or maybe he was hungry enough that anything would taste great. "What do you mean?"

"Where are you from?"

Andy chewed some more, then swallowed. "Kentucky."

Missy stopped with the fork inches from her mouth. She looked in his direction, but her gaze did not quite meet his eyes. She was attractive with small, soft features. At first glance, one would think her vulnerable and defenseless, but after spending a mere hour with her, Andy knew better. There was a strength about her, a resolve that could only come from a past peppered with trial and testing. "And how did you get from Kentucky to the drainage pipe?"

Andy swallowed again. "Yeah, the drainage pipe. That's a long story."

She leaned forward. "We're going to Maine. We're in Pennsylvania. We have a lot of time."

"How 'bout you first?"

She stared in his direction for a handful of seconds as if weighing his request, her eyes never staying in one spot longer than a few moments. "Okay. But then you have to tell me yours. That's the deal."

"Deal."

Missy pushed some eggs around on her plate, finally got some on her fork, and lifted it to her mouth. She chewed while her eyes bounced all around Andy's face but never landed on it. As cruel as it seemed, he was thankful she was blind. If she could see him for what he was, she would avoid his face intentionally, and that would hurt him.

Finally, she said, "I was born in Virginia, but my dad left us shortly after I came onto the scene. I was born seeing, in case you're wondering. He left just because I was here, because I existed, not because I was blind. He never wanted kids. He wasn't dad material. A year later, my mom hooked up with Ron, a real winner. He moved us to Maryland to be closer to his family. Ron was a jerk. He beat my mom and me on a regular basis. She always made excuses for him and mostly blamed his fits of anger on me. If I'd just shut up, everything would be okay, but I talked too much. My talking irritated him, angered him, and he took it out on us by using us for punching bags." She shrugged. "So it was my fault."

Andy spread butter on his toast and took a bite.

"You still with me, big guy?"

"Go on. I'm listening."

"This went on until I was seven. Beatings almost every day."

"Didn't anyone notice?"

"Mom homeschooled me. We rarely left the house." She paused to take another bite of her eggs and wash them down with water. "One day Ron came home in a particularly bad mood. I found out later he'd lost a lot of money on some bet he'd made. He took his anger out on me, beat me nearly senseless, then threw me down the steps. I lived, obviously, but," she snapped her fingers, "just like that the lights went out and never came back on."

Andy sat in silence. Anger brought heat to his cheeks. "How old are you now, Missy?"

"Twenty-one."

She'd been blind for thirteen years. Thirteen years of wandering a dark earth.

"That woke my mom up. She had some notion he'd change until then. That's when she finally realized dear old Ron was never going to change. His behavior would only get worse until one of us wound up dead. When I got out of the hospital, she said Ron had been arrested and would spend a long time in jail. We moved to Pittsburgh. She got herself cleaned up too. Got a job, got us a house. She became a good mom. Not great, but good."

Missy stopped like she had no more to say.

"How did you wind up on the road, hitchhiking from Pittsburgh?" Andy asked.

Outside the diner, an engine revved, a deep throaty rumble

that vibrated all the way into the booth. Andy parted the blinds and peered through the slats. "You stay here," he said.

He slid out of the seat, donned his Stetson, and walked to the door of the diner. Missy followed him, her white stick tapping the tiled floor. Andy pushed through the door and stood just outside the diner, arms hanging loosely at his sides, shoulders relaxed. The storm clouds had inched closer, now hovering almost directly above the diner. Their empty promise sneered at the struggling life below. Five pickups, all with oversized tires and jacked up with diesel exhausts spouting black smoke, waited in the parking lot. One of them he recognized as Colin's. So he had left them where he knew they would be so he could round up some friends to go back and take care of the freaks.

Andy turned to Missy. "Get back inside, okay?" He didn't want her to hear what was about to happen. For the second time that morning, he was glad she was blind.

Chapter 4

One of the trucks, an old faded blue Dodge, revved its engine, a full-throated guttural rumble that vibrated in Andy's chest like thunder. Andy tensed his muscles and clenched his fist. He drew in a deep breath of the stale, dry air.

The Dodge growled again, this time so fiercely that it rocked back and forth on its suspension. The earth seemed to shudder beneath Andy's feet. Then another pickup, a dusty Chevy, blasted its air horn. Andy flinched.

The door of Colin's truck opened, and Colin climbed down from the elevated seat. The smirk on his face was anything but friendly. Slowly, hands in the pockets of his jeans, he approached Andy. He appeared relaxed, but under his T-shirt his muscles were taut.

Standing before Andy, Colin smiled, then laughed. "You seem a bit jittery there, cowboy. You all right?"

Andy said nothing. He was not going to be baited by this punk.

Colin leaned to one side and lifted his eyebrows at Andy. "You a tough guy, huh?"

Again, Andy did not answer. He looked past Colin at the line of trucks. One by one, the other drivers climbed down from their seats. Some held baseball bats, one gripped a two-by-four, another a crowbar. They did not come to have a conversation with Andy; they did not come to offer empty threats in an attempt to scare him off. They came to maim and kill.

"I heard about the hurtin' you put on my buddies back in Mason."

Mason. So that was the name of the town. It meant nothing to Andy.

"I hear it was quite the show. Put 'em all in the hospital."

Colin positioned himself so he was directly in Andy's line of sight. Andy finally met the punk's eyes. They were eyes not unlike anybody else's eyes, fully human, and yet there was some "otherness" about them that sent a cold chill down Andy's spine.

"You some kind of special cowboy or something? Maybe military? Special forces before everything hit the fan? Is that it? Now you got some chip on your shoulder?"

The door of the diner opened and closed behind Andy. Colin's eyes shifted and looked past Andy.

Andy turned his head a little.

"Missy, please, go back inside."

A hand fell on Andy's left shoulder, bigger and heavier than Missy's. Andy turned and found the older man from inside the diner standing beside him. In the muted light sifting through the clouds, his skin looked even more leathery and worn, like an old, well-used saddle. His shoulders were thick, though, and his muscles hardened from years of laboring. He put something in Andy's hand and spoke in a low, raspy voice. "Take my truck and get the girl outta here."

Andy looked past the man at Missy, standing just outside the door. In this setting, dark clouds above, barren landscape around, and the brood of bloodthirsty vipers behind, she looked frail and lost. She needed protecting. She needed a protector.

"Do it, son." He lifted his eyes to meet Andy's. They were such a light shade of gray they appeared almost translucent. "I'll take care of things here." He winked and smiled, revealing two rows of browning teeth.

Andy hesitated. Colin sneered.

The old man leaned in so only Andy could hear what he said next. "The girl . . . this is about her. All of it. She's something special. Get her outta here. Don't look back and don't come back. No matter what. I got this."

Andy opened his hand and found a set of keys. The old man nodded toward a black Toyota Tundra parked along the side of the diner. "Go now."

Andy hesitated, glanced at Colin and the others. During the brief interaction with the old man, the others had inched closer. They looked hungry, ready to strike.

The old man drilled Andy with a hard stare. "Now, son."

The old man stepped in front of Andy and straightened his spine. Andy backed away, then grabbed Missy's hand and headed for the truck.

"Where you goin', cowboy?" Colin hollered. "We ain't done here."

But Andy and Missy were already near the Toyota. "Can you get in by yourself?" Andy asked.

"Sure can," Missy said.

Andy left her and jumped in behind the wheel, brought the engine to life. A second later, Missy climbed into the passenger seat. In front of the diner, Colin stood statue still, glaring at Andy, that smirk still plastered on his face as if he knew something Andy didn't, as if he knew that just over the horizon, out of sight, waited a hundred pickups and a hundred more bloodthirsty vipers ready to strike, destroy, and devour.

Colin took a step toward the truck, but the old man put his hand on the younger man's chest and stopped him. Andy hit the gas, the rear tires spun in the dusty soil, then finally found traction. The truck lurched forward. As he left the parking lot, he saw the group close in on the old man.

The Toyota hit the road at twenty miles an hour, leaving a plume of dust behind it. As the speedometer needle climbed and the dust settled, Andy checked the rearview mirror. Nausea gripped his stomach tightly. The group of punks had descended on the old man. There were so many of them, and they were in no mood to show mercy.

Andy groaned. He wanted to turn the truck around, get back there, and let his rage loose. But the old man's words bounced around in his head: *The girl . . . this is about her. All of it. She's something special.*

"What is it?" Missy turned her face toward Andy. "What's happening?"

Get her outta here. Don't look back and don't come back.

Andy took his foot off the accelerator and allowed the truck to slow.

"What's going on?"

No matter what. I got this.

It was probably too late now anyway. He'd waited too long.

Before he could answer Missy, two pairs of headlights glowed through the dust like demon eyes.

"Hold on." Andy stomped on the gas pedal.

Chapter 5

Two trucks had broken away from the pack back at the diner and were now in frenzied pursuit. The Toyota had a good engine under the hood—the old man had taken care of it—and it had enough power to keep distance between Andy and Missy and their pursuers. The road lay straight and flat and cut through wasteland for another mile or so. Ahead, Andy could see a leafless tree line. He depressed the accelerator almost to the floor. The speedometer climbed steadily. Fifty, fifty-five, sixty, sixty-five.

Behind them, the pickups held the distance but were unable to close it.

"Are they following us?" Missy's eyes were wide, and the color had drained from her face. She gripped the door handle with her right hand and braced herself against the dashboard with her left hand.

"They are," Andy said. "It'll be okay."

"Can you outrun them?"

"I think so."

"Think so isn't very comforting."

"It's the best I got right now."

A minute later, the truck hit the tree line, and the road curved hard to the left. Andy had to brake hard, locking up the wheels, which caused the bed to fishtail right to left and back again. Missy shrieked and pressed herself against the seat.

Regaining control of the truck, Andy jammed the accelerator to the floor. The rear tires squealed and spun, and the back end fishtailed again. Finally, the tires found traction and the truck lunged forward.

By now, though, the two pickups had closed the gap between them and the Tundra. Before Andy could regain speed, one pickup was on their rear bumper. The collision was sudden and violent, nearly jolting Andy and Missy out of their seats. The truck lurched, the tires skipped and skidded across the blacktop, then found their grip and once again thrust the Tundra onward.

"Are we okay?" Missy's voice was tight and shuddered with fear.

"For now."

"Again. Not comforting."

"Just hold on," Andy said.

The Toyota accelerated again, both pickups on its tail. The road wound around barren trees and through a forest of decomposing leaves and fallen giants. Impossible to gain any kind of real speed. Andy worked the gas and brake as best he could, content now to keep the pursuers off his bumper again.

But they were close. Uncomfortably close. Just twenty or so feet back. Any lapse in his ability to keep speed through the turns and they'd be on him again.

In the rearview mirror, he could see the driver of the pickup directly behind them. He gripped the steering wheel with both hands and leaned forward, baring his teeth. His eyes burned with a hunger for violence.

"How close are they?" Missy asked.

"Close enough."

A tight turn to the right approached, and Andy once again braked hard. As before, the truck's tail end swerved wide, but this time the rear tire caught the lip of the macadam. The wheel spun in the dry dirt along the shoulder, and the truck slowed. It was all the time the pickup behind him needed. The collision came at the driver's side rear panel, along the side of the bed. It pushed the Tundra off the road and spun it counter-clockwise.

Andy saw the tree approaching quickly. The impact slammed his head against the side window, and the lights went out.

. . . .

Missy heard it; she sensed it, even smelled the sudden release of fear pheromones from Andy. But she never saw the approaching impact.

She certainly felt it, though.

The truck jolted violently and spun, inducing a sense of vertigo and nausea that almost made her vomit. She slammed against the door, her head glancing off the window, then was jerked to the left. The sound of crunching metal and skidding tires and the odor of burning rubber and gasoline assaulted her senses.

When the truck finally stopped spinning, it rocked on its suspension, then came to rest. Her head ached where it had hit the window; her shoulder burned. Every attempt to collect her thoughts came up short. Words and images swam in a murky wash of haze. Instinctively, she reached first for her white stick and then for the door handle. She had to get out of there. The other pickups. The punks. Colin's friends.

She rested her hand on the handle and listened. In the distance, but too far off, metal creaked.

"Andy?"

No answer. His breathing was labored. He was alive and still in the truck's cab. She reached across the seat and found him, shoved his mass with her hand. "Andy." Nothing. Was he dead? Unconscious? *Please, God . . . not dead.*

Now footsteps outside the truck, leaves crunching, men talking. Angry voices. Slurred words.

"Get the freak. I'll get the girl."

Missy yanked on the handle, and the door swung open, taking her with it. She stumbled out of the cab and tripped on a branch, landing hard in the leaves. The musty odor of dry leaves burned in her nostrils. Her heart banged hard behind her ribs. Fear gripped her chest and neck and made it difficult to breathe. Quickly, she righted herself, white stick extended in front of her, and took two steps. Went down again. There were too many fallen branches to navigate. She'd never make it out of the maze.

Footsteps approached her, heavy, quick. She swung the stick around in a wide arc and grunted like an animal injured and cornered. A hand caught the stick, ripped it from her hand, and snapped it. The sound resonated through her ears. The stick was her guide, an extension of her arm, her companion for miles and months. The hand then gripped her arm and yanked her up.

"Come here." His voice was gruff and stern, laced with hate.

She tried to struggle, to break free from his grip, but her arm was jerked behind her back and bent upward. Pain stabbed her shoulder. His free arm then wrapped around her waist and pulled her against him. She tried to wrench free.

"Knock it off." His breath smelled of tobacco. His body odor overpowered her, and once again nausea writhed in her stomach like a snake.

The man put his mouth to her ear. He drew in a noisy breath. "We're gonna teach you and your friend a little lesson."

On the other side of the truck, she heard the door open, then something big and loose landed in the leaves. Andy had fallen out of the truck.

"Let's go," another man said.

Missy's captor tightened his hold on her waist, so tight it nearly squeezed the air from her lungs. He lifted her off the ground. "Now we're gonna have some fun. You want that?"

· · · · · · ·

Darkness like he'd never seen outside his dreams enveloped him. Thick, palpable darkness—the kind that infiltrates every pore and orifice, fills it to overflowing and oozes like hot tar. He was floating in it, suspended by the viscous substance, unable to move. Hands grabbed at him, clawed, groped. It was sickening and vulgar. He tried to scream, but when he opened his mouth, the black ooze filled his oral cavity and muffled any call for help.

Alone. No one to help, no one to rescue. He must endure this molestation, this torture, by himself.

From somewhere in the darkness, somewhere far off, a faint whisper swept past him, like the rhythmic susurrations of an autumn wind through leafy trees. Back when the trees still had leaves. Back when the earth was fresh and renewed every spring. Back when rain fell and grass was green. Back before evil had slithered out from under its rock and made earth its home. But as the sound grew louder, the whispering grew closer. There was purpose to it. There was a chant. A name. His name.

Andrew. Andrew. Andrew.

Over and over the voices whispered, chanted until they became a sea of voices joined in a dark, sinister chorus. *An-drew. An-drew.*

A hand found his neck—bony fingers, long, thin, strong. They wrapped around the full circumference of his neck and pulled downward, the fingertips digging into his throat, compressing his trachea, closing his airway.

•••••••

The man carried Missy a short distance and dropped her onto the ground. She dug her heels into the dirt and pushed off until her back found the trunk of a tree. She wrapped her arms around her waist and pulled her knees toward her chest. "What do you want with us?"

"Just to have some fun, pretty thing." He closed in and knelt beside her. His hand touched her face, her cheek, and slid down her neck to her collarbone.

Missy recoiled and lifted a hand to push his away, but he grabbed her wrist and yanked it aside. His hand continued its downward slide to her sternum. Missy wrestled and fell to the side, successfully pulling away from the man's probing hand. But his hand found her hair and jerked her upright again.

"You're gonna take what I give you, and you're gonna like it."

"No!" Missy pulled and writhed. She kicked her feet and tried to roll over. The man was too strong, though. She was no match for his size.

His body odor was stronger now, his sweat laced with acid. His breath reeked of that stale tobacco.

His hands found her shirt and tore the fabric as if it were tissue paper.

Fear raced along her nerves, tightened her muscles. Anger too. Anger like she'd never felt.

Then she smelled it. Something hot, not burning but just hot.

She continued to fight until the man's hand found her face with a closed fist. The blow knocked her sideways, but he wouldn't let her fall.

And then it happened. Intense heat bubbled up from her stomach, into her throat, filled her mouth. Her stomach, chest, and neck muscles all tightened. Such extreme tension she thought they'd tear from their moorings.

A moment later, the world exploded in a flash of light.

·······

Andy fought the feeling of suffocation, of drowning in the oily darkness. He fought it until the hand suddenly lost its grip and fell away.

A spot of light appeared in the far distance and drew near—growing, illuminating everything around him until it was so bright it blinded him.

"Andy." A voice. Distant and muffled.

He was on his butt, his back against something hard. His head throbbed.

"Andy." A woman. Her voice weak, strained. Pity-filled.

As his vision cleared, the naked forest around him came into focus. Dark silhouettes of leafless trees plastered against a gray sky.

"Andy." Missy.

He opened his mouth. "Yeah." The fog that had clouded his mind and blurred his vision cleared enough that he could put a few thoughts together. The pursuers. Colin's guys. They'd run him off the road. Missy was there too. "Missy."

"I'm here. I'm okay." Her voice quaked. She hesitated. "We're both okay."

Andy turned his head and found Missy by his side, her hand on his forehead. Tears wet her cheeks. The left side of her face was red and swollen, the flesh around her eye puffy and dark. Her shirt was torn and littered with broken leaves. She struggled to hold it together with one hand.

"Are you okay?"

"Yes. I am."

Behind them, the three trucks idled. The bed of the Tundra was wrapped partly around the thick trunk of a tree. The other two pickups were empty. Andy looked past Missy and scanned the area. Where were the—

There. On the other side of the Chevy in a small clearing.

Andy pushed up and balanced himself on rubbery legs. He found his Stetson and gave it its rightful place atop his head. He then staggered over to the clearing and stood over the two bodies of their pursuers. Both were covered in deep red burns, their flesh blistered and singed.

"Oh, Missy." He turned his face toward the blind girl who had followed him into the clearing. Tears poured from her eyes. "What did you do?"

Chapter 6

The man sat at the booth in the diner and sipped his coffee. He faced the door, always faced the door. He needed to see who was coming and going. His life depended on it. He sat the mug on the table and studied the back of his hand. The flesh was thin and as wrinkled as crumpled cellophane. Large veins wormed their way between and over thin, birdlike bones. But he was much older than he looked—much older, in fact, than anyone would believe.

He'd seen it all. Literally. Wars. Revolutions. Assassinations. Coups. Kingdoms rise and fall. Presidents come and go. Babies born. Men dying. Weddings, funerals. Tears and laughter. Nothing had escaped him. His life, his existence had been quite fulfilling. And over the years, he'd learned to watch, to observe, to note the ebbs and flows of time, the changing seasons of nature and men. He'd seen men reach the highest, grandest, most lofty positions, and he'd witnessed the birth of destruction, the near end of civilization, the hell on earth that could be unleashed at the beckoning of one man.

But never had he witnessed a time like this. The earth had groaned under the weight of the times. The event that ushered in the final act had slowed the onward march of the world's human population to a painful crawl. But it was necessary, at least from his point of view. It was the only way forward.

The man sipped his coffee again and scanned the diner. The waitress, a middle-aged graying brunette, wiped down the counter. Another patron sat a few booths away, his back to the man. He, too, faced the door. Most folks did nowadays. One couldn't be too careful. Even though it had been ten years since The Taking (what most people called The Event), law enforcement hadn't gotten back up to full speed. Most of the country outside the major metropolitan areas had become the new Wild West. Men protected themselves and their loved ones. Few looked out for others. Commodities were too precious. Folks had become self-focused, withdrawing inside themselves like turtles pulling back into their shells for protection and privacy.

But this was as it should be. If folks thought The Taking was bad, they had no idea how bad the world would become.

He wasn't here for mankind. They'd have to fend for themselves. No, he was here for one person in particular. One person whose existence had been carefully planned. One person who was here at the perfect time for a specific purpose.

For such a time as this.

One person—a just person—who had learned the difficult way of walking by faith.

The just shall live by faith.

The girl. She had no idea yet, and he wasn't sure she would understand until the moment arrived, but the fate of the world hung on her ability to travel safely to her destination. That's why they had recruited her travel companion. He was worthy of such a task. But he had so much to learn. The man wondered at times if they had chosen correctly. But he'd wondered that before, many times, only to discover time and time again that they always chose correctly.

The man finished his coffee, dropped a few bills on the table, and left the diner. He had places to go. He needed to stay ahead of the girl and her companion.

·······

In the same diner, at the same time, sat another man. Nursing his own coffee. Fingering a few sugar packets and staring at a scratch that cut a deep groove in the surface of the table. He was an outlaw of sorts. A renegade. Wanted, but not wanted by anyone in particular. To most, he was invisible. Just another traveler making his way across the country. Alone. And wanting to be left alone.

Folks had changed since The Event. The care they once had shown for each other had turned to greed for some, but for most, it had been replaced by indifference. Much of life—the life they used to love and enjoy—didn't matter anymore. They cared for themselves now. Minded their own business. Stayed out of each other's way.

He liked it this way. He could remain unnoticed. He could move about without being bothered or questioned or followed. Folks just didn't care about him. He was unimportant.

But they were wrong.

He was very important. They had no idea how important. He was part of a greater plan, part of something much larger than himself or his own miserable existence.

It was all about the girl. She too was important. Very important. More important, in fact, than he was. And he was going to destroy her.

The man picked up a sugar packet and turned it over and over in his hand. He then tore the top off and allowed the grains to spill out onto the table. With his index finger, he drew a circle in the fine white granules. The girl's days were like the grains of sugar. Dissolvable. So easily wiped out. He moved his hand across the table, palm down, and scattered the grains.

He would find her, of course. Eventually. Like a wolf tracking sheep. And then he would kill her. He might even take his time, have a little fun first. And why not? There was little in this life to enjoy, little in this world to enjoy. If the opportunity came to squeeze a little pleasure from such a wretched place . . . why not?

Chapter 7

Missy pressed herself against the truck's door and grasped the seat belt crossing her chest with both hands. Andy had given her an old pullover stuffed behind the driver's side seat. It smelled of oil and grease and was a bit large for her frame but gave her the cover she needed. The window rattled against her head as the truck barreled down the road. They'd taken one of the pickups, and it carried the scent of the man who tried to rape her. Tobacco and body odor. The smell knotted her stomach.

Andy had tried to pry out of her what had happened while he'd been unconscious, but she didn't know. She didn't. At least she couldn't explain it in any terms he could understand. She told him about the assault and her efforts to fight the man off. But after that . . . she just couldn't say.

She now feared herself. Maybe more so than she feared any man. Andy had described to her the dead bodies in the clearing. But she couldn't give him sensible answers as to how they came to be like that. Had she done it? If so, how? Or had they been struck by lightning? Had she been struck as well? Flash rainfalls were rare but not unheard of since The Event. Thunderstorms were even more rare.

She recalled little. She'd felt intense burning in her mouth and throat along with a tightening in her abdomen and chest so severe she thought she'd vomit. Then she'd blacked out; she wasn't even sure for how long. When she became aware again, she was still standing, her entire body tingling like it had conducted a thousand volts of electricity. She felt no pain, though. Soon after that, Andy stirred, and she felt her way across the rough terrain to where he lay against the tree.

Missy could take the odor in the truck's cab no longer and rolled down the window.

"You okay?" Andy said.

"Just need some air."

The truck rattled and knocked around on the rough pavement. Since The Event, nothing had been repaired. Potholes took over whole sections of road. Some roads had almost fully deteriorated and returned to a gravel-like state.

"You sure you're okay?"

"I'm not sure. But . . . can we change the subject?" The thought of what had happened, what she had quite possibly done, was too much to ponder. Her mind needed a rest.

"Sure. You didn't finish your story back there at the diner. You left Pittsburgh."

Yes, she left Pittsburgh. Not by choice. The memory of Dear Old Ron put a knot in her stomach. "Ron got out of prison early. He knew some guys who knew some guys who knew the district attorney, or something like that. He came up for early release and, surprise, Ron was on the loose again."

"Nothing you two could do about it?"

"Nope. My mom talked to our lawyer, pleaded our case, but his hands were tied too. The district attorney had called in a few favors. Those favors apparently reached all the way to the governor. We were outnumbered and outranked."

"So you ran."

"Not at first. Ron was on parole. We knew he had to be on his best behavior. One slipup and he'd be back in the can, and there wouldn't be anything anyone could do about it. So we hunkered down and lived as normally as we could."

But that normalcy only lasted so long. Then everything changed. Memories of that day and her mother's untimely death rolled through Missy's mind. The knot was now in her throat. She needed to change the subject again. Talk about something not so personal.

"How much fuel do we have?"

"'Bout three-quarters of a tank."

"Where do you think they got it?" It had been over a decade since The Event, and most, if not all, the gas stations had been pumped dry within a few years. There simply was not enough manpower to produce gasoline fast enough and get it to the consumer. Some folks had converted their vehicle's engine to run on methane, some on ethanol, some on vegetable oil. But folks mostly looked out for themselves, and unless one had mechanical skills and knowledge, he either scavenged for gasoline, bought it on the black market (usually at a very personal price), or took to bicycling. Missy had heard of people selling themselves for sex, consigning their children to indentured slavery, and bartering most of their earthly goods for a few gallons of fuel. In the past five years, though, most of the refineries had been resurrected, and gas had become available again on a limited basis and mostly around more densely populated areas.

"Don't know. Must be a gas station around here somewhere."

She was about to inquire about the price of gas when Andy grunted.

"What is it?"

"Hitchhiker."

Missy pushed away from the door and sat upright in the seat. "Man? Woman?"

"A guy. Young."

"Are you going to stop?"

"Nope."

"Why not?"

"We can't trust him."

"How do you know?"

"I don't. But we can't take any chances."

Missy turned her face toward Andy. She knew he was being protective of her, but she also knew what it was like to be out there by herself. "Please stop."

Andy slowed the truck. "Why?"

"We need to help him, to do what we can to keep our humanity. I've been this guy many times, and someone usually stopped to give me a lift."

"Usually," Andy said. The truck stopped. Andy was silent for a moment. "I guess he looks innocent enough. But any weird stuff, anything I'm uncomfortable with, and he goes."

Missy smiled. "I'm a good judge of character."

"You are?"

"Yes. Why?"

"I'm not so sure about the company you've been keeping lately."

· · · · · · ·

The guy was young, late teens or early twenties, thin, with deep-set eyes and sunken cheeks. His hair hung to his shoulders, and a few weeks' worth of growth covered the lower half of his face. Missy slid over on the bench, and the newcomer climbed into the cab after stowing his duffel bag behind the seat.

"Thanks for the ride. I have no idea how far I've walked."

"Where you headed?" Andy asked.

"Anywhere. Nowhere." He laughed. "Everywhere."

Missy reached for the seat belt and fastened it around her waist. "A man with purpose. I like that."

The hitchhiker smirked. "That I am not. Name's Trevor." He reached out his hand to shake Missy's. When she didn't respond, Trevor glanced at Andy, then said, "I'm sorry. I didn't realize . . ."

"I'm blind. I'm also Missy."

"Nice to meet you, Missy." He took her hand and shook it, then extended his hand to Andy.

Andy didn't like this kid. He had no reason not to. Trevor seemed innocent and friendly enough, but there was a feeling in Andy's gut that told him not to trust this stranger. Not yet, anyway.

Andy took Trevor's hand in a firmer than necessary grip. "Andy." When he turned his face fully toward Trevor, he saw the look of disgust that passed through the kid's eyes, and he didn't miss the subtle shift in body posture that inched Trevor closer to the door.

Andy shifted the truck into drive and hit the gas. They had time to make up and distance to cover while they had gas in the tank. Plus, he wondered if Colin and what was left of his minions might come looking for their friends. When they found them, Andy wanted to be miles away.

As he drove, Andy kept his gaze on the road. They'd broken free of the forest, and the road now cut a straight path through terrain that was once acres of fertile fields—corn, soy, wheat— but now lay barren and wasted. Dry as a sun-scorched bone. The road's condition was no better here than in the forest, though, and he had to pay close attention to the potholes and patches of crumbling pavement that riddled the way.

They sat in uncomfortable silence for several minutes before Andy said, "Where are you from, Trevor?"

"Florida."

Missy turned her face toward him. "Florida? Did you walk all this way?"

"Most of it. Hitched some of it, but mostly walked."

"How long?" Missy asked.

"How long what?"

"How long have you been traveling?"

"Since it happened."

Missy turned her face toward the windshield. "Ten years."

"Yup. I was nine. That first year, you know, when things were the worst, we—I—went into hiding. Then when the craziness stopped . . . you know, when the government went back to something that resembled normal, we spent another year in hiding because most people were still crazy."

"It was bad," Missy said.

"Bad seems tame compared to what I saw."

A memory flashed through Andy's mind. More bits and pieces of images than anything else. Fire. Yelling. Suffocation. And smoke. So much smoke. Filling his lungs. Struggling to breathe. Grasping at anything that might lift him above the smoke line. Then the panic: he was dying.

He gripped the steering wheel tighter. Trevor was still talking.

". . . Took me three years to get out of Florida. I've camped out in several places since then. Spent almost a year in North Carolina. Some of the cities there are almost back to normal."

They drove in silence again. Andy could tell Missy was thinking about something, mulling something over. He glanced at her. She was chewing on her bottom lip.

"You said *we*."

"We?" Trevor said.

"Yeah. You said *we* went into hiding."

Ahead, a small town lay on the horizon.

"Oh, yeah. My mom and me. She was with me the first four years."

Missy hesitated, then asked, "What happened?"

"She, uh, got sick. We were in South Carolina, pretty much the middle of nowhere. I went for help, tried to find a town with a pharmacy or hospital, anything, but there was nothing. By the time I returned, she had . . . she, uh . . ."

Missy reached for Trevor's hand and found it. "It's okay. I know. I lost my mom soon after it happened."

Again, a memory was there, stabbing Andy's mind. His mother reaching for him, her black-stained face twisted in agony. The animals were there too. The rats. Scurrying here and there, climbing over one another. The floor moved with them.

The town proved to be mostly empty. A few cars were parked outside a small grocery store. Most of the homes looked abandoned. The town hadn't been touched yet by the rebuilding efforts. These were folks intent on pushing through and surviving on their own without the aid of the government or any of the relief organizations that had popped up. As they drove past the store, a man stepped out and made eye contact with Andy. He then sized up the truck from front to back. As they rolled past, Andy checked his mirrors. The man still stood outside the store, hands in his pockets, watching the truck.

"Hey, you know what?" A hint of excitement tinted Trevor's voice.

Missy said, "No, what?"

"Do you like to read?"

"Well, I—"

"Braille. Can you read braille?"

Missy's eyes widened. "A little. Yeah."

Trevor reached behind the seat and fished something from his duffel bag. It was a thick hardback book. "Here." He set it on Missy's lap. "*Pride and Prejudice.*"

Missy opened the book and ran her fingers over the textured pages. She giggled. "How in the world did you get this?"

"My mom was blind. Since she was seven. That was her favorite book."

Missy flipped the book to the cover and slid her fingers over the raised title. "Oh, I love this story too." She reached for Trevor's hand, and he let her have it. "Thank you so much. Are you sure, though? It was your mother's."

"She'd want it to be read. I have no use for it other than to remember her. And I have lots of memories that help with that."

Missy turned her face toward Andy and held up the book. "What do you think of this, huh? Aren't we fortunate to have picked up this young man?"

"We sure are," Andy said, though he meant not a word of it. That feeling was there again; something didn't sit right with him about Trevor.

Trevor glanced at Andy and smiled.

Andy wanted to punch him in the mouth.

Chapter 8

The gymnasium of the old high school had been turned into a shelter. Andy found out that city officials had shut down St. Vincent's Catholic High School soon after The Event and never reopened it. The kids were funneled to either the local public school or other private schools in the area. Many parents also took to homeschooling their children.

With its high ceilings and cavernous space, the gym seemed much larger than it was. Sleeping bags, cots, blankets, and pillows covered almost every square foot of floor space. Piles of clothes sat here and there, some neatly folded, some strewn about like a mishmash of debris after a garment factory explosion.

Andy returned to Trevor and Missy standing by the door. Missy held on to Trevor's arm. She looked smaller than usual, fragile. Andy didn't like the chummy Trevor; something about him still didn't click.

"Tim said we can take the spot over there by the bathrooms." Andy pointed across the gym to one of the only open areas on the floor. "There are showers in the locker rooms. Clothes in boxes at either end of the gym. He said we can help ourselves."

Missy's eyes widened. "Tim?"

"The priest," Andy said. "He runs this place."

Missy turned her head from side to side. The constant chatter in the large room was background noise Andy hadn't even noticed until this moment. "So many people," she said. "Where did they all come from?"

"Tim said most of them are travelers. Homeless, wandering from town to town. Need a place to stay for the night, some for more. He said some have been here for months. A few for years."

Missy turned her face toward Trevor. "Like us."

Trevor patted her arm. "That's right, little sister. Like us."

Trevor had taken to calling Missy "little sister," and it bugged Andy. "We should head over there. Tim has some blankets we can use for the night. First thing in the morning, we'll hit the road again."

"Can't we stay a few days?" Trevor inclined his head toward Missy. "I think we could all use the rest."

Andy tightened his jaw. "You can stay if you like, Trevor, but Missy and I need to keep moving."

"Maybe just one day," Missy said.

Trevor smiled at Andy. It wasn't a sinister smile, nor did it convey any sense of malice or arrogance, but Andy didn't like it. He wanted to tell the tagalong to beat it, go back to wherever he came from or keep heading toward wherever he was going before they picked him up. But Missy liked Trevor. To run him off would alienate her, and he couldn't do that. The old man's words at the diner came back to him:

The girl . . . this is about her. All of it. She's something special.

Something special.

Andy believed it too. She was special. He didn't know how or what it all meant, but there was something different about her, something unique and innocent yet powerful. Besides all that, he genuinely liked Missy, maybe even more than liked her. Whether he had intended it or not—he hadn't—and whether he wanted it or not—he didn't—she'd opened a room in his heart he thought he'd locked forever. He cared for her, although he wasn't sure if it was in a little-sister kind of way or something more than that.

Regardless, he'd have to tolerate Trevor for now. If he was the loser Andy thought he was, sooner or later it would surface, and Missy would discover it for herself. Until that time, Andy would watch him. Missy's safety was his responsibility, and he would do whatever was needed to protect her.

After helping themselves to some clean clothes, they went to the far corner of the gym and spread out the blankets the priest had supplied. Missy sat with her back against the wall, and Andy lowered himself next to her.

"Hey, I'm gonna go look around, okay?" Trevor said.

Missy smiled. "Sure."

Andy said nothing. Maybe Trevor would get lost and not return at all.

Trevor tapped the top of Missy's head. "Be back in a few."

Andy watched as Trevor wove around and through a maze of makeshift beds and living spaces.

"He's nice, isn't he?" Missy said.

Andy didn't answer.

"You don't like him."

"It's not that I don't like him," Andy said. "We don't know him. Not really." On the far side of the gym, near the door to the outside world, Trevor shook hands with another man of about the same age and build, then hugged him, slapping the guy hard on the back. "I don't trust him. Not yet."

"He seems trustworthy."

Trevor and the other guy stood close, their faces just inches apart. Trevor motioned toward the door.

"I think it's too early to tell."

Trevor glanced over his shoulder at Andy and Missy, noticed he was being watched, and threw Andy a smile and nod.

Andy scanned the room. Most of the inhabitants were older and appeared weak. They'd probably been on the road the entire ten years since The Event, wandering about in a nomadic trance. Following those initial days, weeks, and months, those who had means re-established themselves in the new world. Those who couldn't became wanderers—like Trevor—moving from shelter to shelter, finding beds where they could, transportation where it appeared, food where it was available. News sources had estimated that a full forty percent of the country was jobless, and of that group nearly seventy-five percent were homeless.

Trevor shook his friend's hand again, turned, and zigzagged through the sea of cots and blankets. He arrived smiling, thumbs hooked in the pockets of his jeans. "Hey, Missy, come with me. I want you to meet someone."

"Who is he?" Andy asked.

"His name's Jordan. He's an old friend of mine from North Carolina." Trevor turned his attention back to Missy. "You'll like him, Missy. He saved my life once near Greensboro."

Missy turned her face toward Andy as if seeking his approval, but Andy said nothing. He didn't want her to go, but if he balked, she'd go anyway, and he'd be left looking like the jerk.

When he didn't respond, Missy extended her hand toward Trevor. "Okay. Sure."

Trevor grasped her hand and pulled her to her feet. He took her by the arm and led her through the room. Andy watched every step.

At the far end of the gym, Trevor made introductions, and Missy shook the new guy's hand. He smiled and dipped his head so he could look into her eyes. Had Trevor told him Missy was blind?

Trevor turned and glanced at Andy, then redirected his eyes across the gym, toward the end where one of the basketball hoops hung suspended from the ceiling. Andy followed his gaze and found a young boy no more than six or seven standing in the middle of a circle of sleeping bags. His worn, faded shirt hung loosely on his shoulders. His hair was mussed and shaggy. The boy stared at Andy, a blank expression on his face. Andy expected the kid to begin to cry and point, directing the attention of the entire room to the freak by the bathrooms. But he did neither. Instead, he lifted a small hand and gave a weak wave.

Andy tipped his hat to the boy and smiled, then turned back, looking for Missy. But she was gone. Trevor and his friend were gone too.

Andy stood, scanned the room. His heart thumped hard and fast all the way up to his neck. His palms went sweaty. He'd lost her.

Andy hurried through the room, stepping over sleeping bags and around cots. A man his size moving at such a rate drew attention. Folks whispered and pointed. If he had any hope of blending in and remaining invisible to people who themselves had been invisible, he was only fooling himself.

Finally, he made it to where the threesome had been standing. A small man with deeply rutted skin and a spotty gray beard met his eyes.

"Did you see where they went?" Andy asked.

"Two men and a woman?"

"Yes."

The man pointed out the door, to the darkening evening.

Andy cursed. He'd lost her.

． ． ． ． ． ． ．

The man enjoyed watching the events unfold. A master of blending in, he took pleasure in his voyeuristic endeavors. The kid was doing okay so far. He was following the plan, which was all the man could ask at this time.

Panic had overcome the freak and it amused the man. But so much more was to come. His panic would turn to fear, then to anger, then to rage. And that rage would be the end of him and the girl. He would self-destruct and take the girl with him. Genius, really. He was so ripe for the picking. A little push here, a harder push there—that's all it would take. His true nature was itching to bust out and have its way.

The man sat back against the wall and watched the freak move through the crowd. People stared and murmured. He was such a monster; everyone could see it.

He smiled and felt a certain sense of elation. The kid had turned out to be vulnerable and pliable. When the time came, he would prove useful. And disposable.

Chapter 9

The sun slid toward the western horizon. A smattering of pink clouds dotted the purplish sky. If he weren't in this place at this exact moment, Andy would stop for a moment and admire the handiwork.

But this was no time for gawking at a sunset. Missy was gone. Outside, a few stragglers mulled around aimlessly, nursing cigarettes. One couple argued loudly; two small children cowered behind their mother.

But there was no Missy. No Trevor. No Jordan. The truck was still there, parked about twenty yards away. They couldn't have gone far.

Andy rushed around to the left of the building. He'd circle the entire school and scan the fields surrounding it. If they were out there, he'd find them. It had been only minutes since Trevor had directed his gaze away from them.

· · · · · · ·

"You should come with us," Jordan said. He had a nice voice, smooth and friendly. His handshake had been firm but not too strong. Missy could tell a lot by someone's voice or handshake.

"Yeah, we could break out and make our own path." Trevor touched Missy's arm. "Come with us, Missy."

"But what about Andy? He—"

"What about him?" Trevor's voice held no sharp edges. He was always kind. "He'll be fine on his own. He's a big guy, can take care of himself."

"I need to go north."

"We'll go north."

"Yeah," Jordan said. "All the way to Maine. I've been there. I know the way."

Missy bit her lip. Though she'd only known Trevor a day, she trusted him. Something about the way he spoke, his gentle ways—like a big brother she didn't know she had who finally walked into her life and picked up right where they'd left off.

"Look," Trevor said. "Did Andy invite you to join him? Did he want you along?"

He hadn't. In fact, he'd balked at her tagging along. He would have sent her on her way all alone if she hadn't insisted.

"No."

Trevor touched Missy's cheek. His hand was soft. "I'll protect you, little sister. I won't ever leave you alone. Andy's cool and all, but I think he's looking out for himself first. There's something he has to do, and you're in the way."

"You wanna go north?" Jordan said. "We're the duo to get you there."

....

Andy headed around the west side of the school; his heart still raced, sweat dotted his forehead. When he found them—

There they were. All three of them. Missy had her back to the brick wall. Trevor stood beside her. Jordan faced them, hands in his pockets.

Anger clawed into Andy's chest. He wanted to lift Trevor by his skinny neck and pin him to the wall. But that would do no good. They hadn't seen him yet. He stepped quickly, purposely keeping his hands loose. He drew in a deep breath, held it for a second, then slowly let it go.

When Andy was about thirty feet away, Jordan spotted him.

"Uh-oh."

Trevor turned to face Andy, a smug smile curling the corners of his mouth.

Andy stopped ten feet away and forced his voice to sound calm. He didn't want to cue Missy he was upset. "Hey, what're you guys doing out here?"

Missy spoke first. "I asked them if we could get some fresh air. It was getting stuffy in there."

Andy shifted his eyes between Trevor and Jordan. Both stared back at him, cocky, careless.

"Missy, why don't you come back inside?" Andy hoped she heard the concern in his voice and not the irritation. "We need to be careful, you know?"

Missy hesitated. Her eyes darted around his face. Her expression was defiant. "I'd like to stay out here a little while longer."

"We'll take good care of her, boss," Jordan said. He was a thin guy, tall and scrawny. The greasy type. Sharp lines to his face. Dark hair pulled back into a bun.

"Relax, Andy," Trevor said. "You're among friends."

"Missy, please." Andy's concern was real now. These guys set off so many alarms in his gut. "Come inside. You should probably get showered for the night, you know?" He stepped closer, reached past Trevor, and put his hand on Missy's shoulder, hoping she would sense his concern through his touch. "Please."

Missy's face relaxed. "Okay. It's probably best. I'm filthy and tired anyway."

Andy shot Trevor and Jordan a look that warned them not to follow. He took Missy by the arm and gently led her back to the gymnasium.

．．．．．．．

Missy slept on a stack of folded blankets while Andy sat with his back against the wall. He'd taken a quick shower while Missy was in the women's locker room and returned to the gym before she arrived. The lights in the gym had been turned off at ten, and the only illumination now was the moon filtering in through the rectangular windows near the ceiling. The hushed sounds of nearly a hundred people sleeping or whispering quietly filled the gym. Andy had not been able to locate Trevor or Jordan since the lights had been turned off. He assumed they were in the gym somewhere, but they hadn't made themselves known since Andy had given them the warning look.

Andy was determined to stay awake through the night, watching over Missy like a shepherd guards his sheep. The wolves were out there, and he needed to protect her, to keep her from harm.

·······

The man had little difficulty seeing in the dark. He had embraced the darkness at an early age and had found comfort there, freedom even. The freak was still awake, his mind churning. He was afraid. He'd never admit it, but the man could tell. Fear was obvious to anyone who knew what he was looking for.

The man sat across the gym from the freak. Far enough away to remain unnoticed but close enough to do what he'd come to do.

And he'd come to do what he did best: destroy.

·······

Andy found some comfort in the freedom darkness allowed him. He could move about without staring eyes, whispers, and frightened looks. In the darkness, he was no different from anyone else. Except he was different, wasn't he? His mangled exterior reflected the state of his soul. There was darkness there too. He knew it, felt it, fought it every day. At times, though, he wanted to embrace it. The pull was so strong, in fact, that resisting it became almost nonsensical. A futile effort. Like a wolf resisting the natural instincts and desires of his . . . wolf-ness.

Andy looked at Missy sleeping peacefully. She was an attractive girl. Woman, really. Sweet too. And innocent. Her innocence stirred something within him, something more than a protective concern that any big brother might have for his sister. Suddenly, a thought entered his mind. He could have her. He could earn her trust, earn her respect. She would grow to love him. She could be his.

Or he could skip all the relationship struggles and just force himself on her. It would be so easy. And he could do it now. He wanted to. And maybe she wanted it too.

Andy shook his head and rubbed his eyes. Where had those thoughts come from? He forced them from his mind. He would never hurt Missy like that. She meant too much to him. She trusted him. It was his duty to protect her, not use her.

Sometime after midnight, Andy's eyelids grew heavy. Keeping them open became more difficult as if someone had sneaked in and tied fishing weights to them, and no matter how hard he struggled to fight the pull, he couldn't keep them open.

Several times, he allowed his eyelids to fall only to flip them open when he realized he'd become unaware of them being closed. Sleep had slipped in unnoticed. This tug-of-war went on for over an hour until Andy finally lost touch with his will and drifted along on the sea of slumber, riding the dark waters into the darker night.

And there he dreamed of monsters, beasts, and monstrosities of all kinds, surfacing in the waves and groping at his limbs. He tried to fight them off, to free himself from their attack, but it was useless. They came at him with such fury and intensity, with such lust for violence and gore. They wanted not only to torment him but also to claim him as their own, to make him one of them. He knew this.

As the night wore on and the waters churned, the assault intensified until the waves became flames and the creatures became images of his mother. She spoke to him beyond the black veil of death. Her voice was strained and edged with urgency.

"The girl. This is about her. All of it. She's something special. Andrew, she's something special. You must protect her."

The fire roared louder and louder until it drowned out his mother's voice.

Then he was on the sea again, riding the crests and troughs of the black water. Something loomed beneath him. He couldn't see it but he could sense it. Menacing. Gliding past him silently, a few feet from the surface. It would strike at any moment and snatch him, pull him down to depths he could never escape. Only a matter of time . . .

Andy awoke with a startle. The first beams of early morning sunlight filtered through the windows and cast the room in an orange tint. People milled around with bedheads and sleep-glazed eyes. The kid who last night waved at Andy stood in the same spot and watched him with curiosity.

Andy rubbed his eyes, ran his fingers through his hair.

Missy was gone. Again.

Chapter 10

Andy stood and shook the fog from his head, wiped the sleep from his eyes. He looked over the room, noting every sleeping area, every person rummaging about. He scanned the entire room twice. No Missy. No Trevor or Jordan either.

Stepping his way through the crowded room, careful not to plant a foot on any sleeper, he crossed the open space as quickly as possible. Maybe they were outside again. Catching some fresh air. He wished Missy would stop leaving him like that. At the doorway, he paused and surveyed the property surrounding the school. Across the street lay a vast expanse of open field, a flat run of brown grass, and beyond that a barren forest. The sun was awake. The sky was clear and blue.

But there was no Missy. Andy adjusted the Stetson on his head and ran left. He'd circle the building. Maybe they'd gone for a walk. Behind the school was a playground area and beyond that more barren forest. The school sat about a mile outside the town on a campus that must have been beautiful at one time. Now it was unfertile and bleak, browns and grays everywhere.

Andy circled the perimeter of the building and returned to the gym door. Maybe they were still inside. Maybe they'd decided to explore the rest of the school. Tim had told him last night that the classroom wings of the building were off limits, but that it didn't stop curious guests from finding a way in.

And that's when he noticed the empty space where the truck had been parked. Once again, anger clawed into Andy's chest. He felt betrayed. How could she leave him? How could she take their truck and abandon him? He removed his hat and ran his fingers through his hair, then rubbed the stubble on his chin.

A voice from behind startled him. "You lookin' for the girl?"

Andy spun around. The voice belonged to a girl, no more than thirteen or fourteen. She was thin and bony, her hair long and tangled. She wore a faded black Twenty One Pilots T-shirt and jeans with a hole in the right knee. Over her left shoulder, she carried a black backpack. "Yes. Did you see them leave?"

"Yup."

She shoved her hands into her pockets and tilted her head to one side.

"And? Did you see which way they went?"

"Yup."

Andy took a step closer to the girl, but she held her ground and lifted her chin, held him with narrowed eyes.

"What do you want?" Andy said.

"To go with you."

Andy took another step closer. "I can't take you with me. I don't even have a vehicle."

"I can get one."

"I'm a freak."

She smiled. "I can see that. And you don't scare me."

"How old are you?"

"Thirteen."

"Got parents?"

"Nope."

"You're on your own?"

"Yup. Have been since I was ten."

Andy surveyed the growing crowd around the school. The occupants were awakening and making their way outside for air and sunshine. He didn't have time for this.

"You can get a car?"

"Better than that." She ran her eyes over the parking lot. "How about an SUV?"

Andy crossed his arms. He didn't want to get involved with this girl. He didn't need her tagging along, slowing things down. He didn't need more responsibility. He had one responsibility—Missy—and look how that turned out.

"I'm useful," the girl said. "You'll see that you need me." She looked to her right and stared down the road. "Besides, we're losing time. They're getting farther and farther away. So what's it gonna be, freak-show?"

She was right. She had his back against a wall with few options. "Fine."

"Great. Follow me." The girl headed across the dried lawn in front of the school and crossed the parking lot to where a late model Ford SUV sat unattended. She tried the driver's side door and found it unlocked. She glanced at Andy. "Careless."

"Wait," Andy said. "You're going to steal it?"

"It's already stolen," she said. "You think someone in there"—she pointed at the school—"bought this with their own money?"

She had a point.

She climbed in behind the wheel and reached under the steering column. "Look, if it'll make you feel better, we'll only borrow it, okay?" She flashed him a crooked smile.

In a few seconds, the girl had the Ford running. The engine hummed. She motioned to the passenger seat. "Hop in."

Andy shook his head. "No way. Move over. I drive or this is a no-go."

"We're wasting time."

"Move over."

The girl hesitated, then climbed over the center console and planted herself in the passenger seat.

Andy slid in behind the wheel. "You drive too?"

"Of course. How do you think I got from Nebraska to here?"

Andy put the vehicle in gear and backed out of the parking space. "Which way?"

She pointed east.

Once they were on the road, he said, "What's your name, anyway?"

"Belle."

"Like the Disney character?"

She smiled. "Beauty and the beast."

"That's original."

"Hey, you walked right into it."

"I guess I did."

"So can I call you something other than freak-show?"

"Andy."

"Like the Disney character."

Andy gave her a blank look.

"*Toy Story*? Really? Andy? The little boy and his favorite toy, Sheriff Woody Pride? The cowboy?"

"Nope."

"So you know who the Disney princess is but not the cowboy." She glanced at the Stetson sitting atop his head. "That's revealing."

They drove for several minutes in silence. Belle kept her face toward the window. Andy watched the road but kept scanning the horizon for any sign of the pickup. On either side of the road, the landscape ran for acres in a series of rolling hills covered with browning grass. Occasionally, an abandoned house would appear. Andy paid close attention for hints of life, but rarely were there signs of any.

Finally, Belle said, "Where're you from, Andy?"

"Kentucky."

"Are you a real-life cowboy?"

"I was."

"Did you rope cattle and ride the range?"

Andy shook his head. "Not that kind of cowboy."

"Did you carry a six-shooter?"

"Not that kind either."

"Any gunfights?"

"Nope."

"Any fights at all? Saloon brawls? Punch-outs in dusty towns?"

Andy hesitated. He'd tried to avoid fights but . . . Dean Shannon had started it. Andy never wanted to fight Dean, but the guy wouldn't give up, wouldn't keep his mouth shut. Something had to be done, and once started, it spiraled out of control. Before Andy knew it, Dean was clinging to life, and Andy was no longer welcome at the ranch. "Just one."

"And?"

"And what?"

"Did you win?"

"Nobody wins those kinds of fights. It's not like in the movies."

Belle turned to look out the window. For a long time, she watched the pale earth glide by. Finally, she turned her face from the window and faced him. "Did you lose anyone when everything went crazy?"

She was referring to The Event. He hesitated, studied the shell of an old farmhouse standing in the middle of a desolate field. "My mother."

"I'm sorry." She looked out the window again. "My parents were taken. I was almost four. My aunt had taken me out for the day so my parents could go out to eat. It was their tenth wedding anniversary. They never came home. My aunt knew what had happened. I don't remember any of it. My aunt raised me until I was ten. She died of a heart attack."

"And since then you've been on your own."

"Flyin' solo like Han."

"Han?"

"Solo. *Star Wars*?"

Andy shook his head.

"Wow. You missed out on a lot, didn't you?"

She started to say something more, but Andy hushed her with his hand. "There." About a quarter mile ahead of them. The truck. Missy.

Chapter 11

Missy sat between Trevor and Jordan in the front seat of the truck. Jordan drove. The odor of cigarettes clung to him like an old mildew and reminded Missy of the assault by Colin's friend.

"Do you mind cracking the windows?" she said.

Jordan said, "Sure."

A gust of cool morning air rushed through the cabin, and Missy drew in a long breath to clear her lungs of the heavy nicotine. She reached up to push hair off her forehead and realized her hand was trembling. She didn't like leaving Andy while he was sleeping. She knew he'd tried to stay awake to watch over her, but after a few hours she'd awakened and heard his deep sleep-breathing. The guy had been through so much and was exhausted.

She wanted to believe that leaving was the best thing for him and her. He seemed like the type who did better on his own, making his own time, setting his own course, marching to his own drum. Maybe that was why he balked at allowing her to tag along in the first place.

She probably could move faster with Trevor anyway. She needed to get to Maine as quickly as possible, and for some reason, trouble seemed to follow Andy.

As if he could sense the battle within her or maybe read the tension on her face, Trevor placed his hand on her right knee and said, "You're doing the right thing."

"Am I?"

"Yes. Andy doesn't want you tagging along."

"I noticed it right away," Jordan said.

"He has his own problems to worry about, his own agenda. You're doing him a favor." Trevor slid his hand away from Missy's knee, a few inches farther up her thigh. "We can get you to where you're going."

Missy dropped her hand to her thigh and brushed Trevor's hand away. She wasn't sure if the move was intentional or not but wanted to assume it wasn't. Until this point, Trevor had been nothing but a gentleman, treating her with respect and kindness. He deserved the benefit of the doubt.

Suddenly, the truck's engine whined and the vehicle lunged forward.

Missy reflexively reached for Trevor. "What's going on?"

"Missy." Trevor took her hand and held it tightly. "Hold on. The ride's about to get rough."

Missy tensed her muscles and braced herself against the back of the seat.

Trevor pulled her hand to his chest. He leaned toward her and pressed his face to her ear. "I'll never let go of you."

·······

"They spotted us," Andy said. The truck had increased its speed to put distance between itself and the SUV.

Andy glanced at Belle. "You got your seat belt tight?"

She tugged on it. "Check."

"Hold on."

Andy pressed the gas pedal almost to the floor. The Ford growled and rumbled down the road. He'd lost sight of the truck when it sped over the next rise in the road. When he crested the hill, he caught a glimpse of it before it rounded the next bend.

"C'mon." He massaged the steering wheel, willing the large vehicle to go faster, to close the gap.

Around the bend, the road straightened and leveled for at least a half mile. The truck was up ahead. He'd gained a little ground but not much. He couldn't let them get away. Not now. He might lose Missy for good.

....

"What's happening? Why did we speed up?" Missy's heart thumped in her chest. Jordan drove erratically. He must have been doing a hundred miles an hour.

"It's nothing, little sister," Trevor said. He put his arm around Missy's shoulders and tried to pull her close, but she resisted.

"What's the matter?" he asked.

She pulled farther away and shrugged his arm off her shoulders. "What's going on? Is it Andy?"

"No way," Jordan said. "That dude doesn't care about you enough to come after you."

"Then what's going on?"

"Nothin'. I just want to get moving. There's no cops around here, and the road is great." Jordan paused and Missy felt him shift his weight. He was lying. "Just figured I'd open this thing up a little and let it run."

"You're lying," Missy said. "It's Andy, isn't it?"

Trevor let go of her hand. "Look, yes, someone is following us, okay? But I doubt it's Andy. He isn't going to go through all the trouble of stealing a car and tracking us down to rescue you. He's not the type."

Missy stiffened and turned her face toward her lap.

"Hey." Trevor touched her under the chin. "Listen, I've been around, you know? I've seen and met all types of people. I know his type. He's out for one thing. Himself. Survival. He may act like he cares, but when the pressure is on, his focus turns on himself. I'm sorry."

Missy wanted to believe Trevor, not because of what he said but because she truly liked him, had from the moment he slid into the seat next to her. She wanted to believe him because if he was lying, it meant she'd been duped. But she wasn't sure she could believe him. She'd felt something about Andy, something special. He was different. She wasn't sure how but she sensed it. He was trustworthy and honest. Yes, there was a side to him that he kept hidden, that he battled quietly; she sensed that too, but she had to trust that voice inside her. The voice that was not of this world, that was not bound by temporal things and finite knowledge. That voice guided her, carried her along, kept her from danger.

And right now the voice was telling her to trust Andy. Not Trevor.

"I want you to stop the truck." She said it with as much authority as she could muster.

"No way," said Jordan.

．．．．．．．

Andy depressed the accelerator to the floor. "Let's see what this thing can do."

The truck's engine growled again. Belle stiffened and grabbed her seat belt.

The speedometer's needle climbed steadily, passing seventy, seventy-five, eighty. The road ahead was straight and flat. If Andy was going to gain ground, now was the time to do it.

．．．．．．．

"Oh man," Jordan said. "We gotta go."

The truck accelerated again and pressed Missy into the seat. She had to do something. This wasn't right. "Stop the truck now," she said again. "I want to get out."

Neither of her companions responded, and Jordan did nothing to slow the truck.

"Trevor," she said. "Tell him to stop the truck."

But Trevor said nothing. She felt him next to her, tense and still.

She'd have to take matters into her own hands. With her heart in her throat, she reached for Jordan's right arm and yanked on it.

"Hey! What?" Jordan ripped his arm from her grip and elbowed her in the shoulder. "Knock it off. Trevor, get a grip on her."

Quicker than she could respond, Trevor reached around her and pulled her into his body, pinning both her arms to her sides. She tried to break free, but any effort to break his grip was futile.

·······

The SUV's engine proved much more powerful than the aging pickup's. Andy made ground quickly and closed the gap.

·······

"Let me go," Missy barked.

Trevor squeezed her harder. "Stop it, Missy. This is for your own good. We're protecting you. Can't you see he's obsessed with you?"

"No. Stop the truck." She strained more but could not move Trevor's arms. Instead, she lowered her head and clamped her mouth on his arm.

Trevor yelped and butted Missy hard in the side of the head. Pain thumped in her skull and radiated into her eyes. Trevor did not loosen his grip.

·······

The SUV was a mere ten feet from the truck's rear bumper. Andy thought about ramming it, but he didn't want to upend the truck and take the chance of injuring Missy. The driver, Jordan, was erratic, barely in control. The truck jerked right, then left, swerved in and out of the lane, crossing the center line, then toying with the shoulder.

"Hang on," Jordan said. "I got an idea."

The truck slowed dramatically; the tires locked and screamed across the road's surface. Missy lurched forward. The seat belt dug into her abdomen and hips. Trevor lost his grip on her.

•••••••

The truck's brake lights illuminated, and quicker than Andy could respond, the SUV's front bumper collided with the pickup's rear bumper. A sudden stop, the moan and groan of bending metal. The fracture of shattering glass.

Andy lifted his arm to brace Belle, but it was too late. She flew forward against her seat belt and let out a hideous shriek.

•••••••

The truck then jumped forward, the tires skidding along the asphalt. Missy was whipped back into the seat, her head snapping backward. Pain shot like lightning down her spine.

•••••••

The tail end of the SUV swerved to the right as Andy lost control. It continued to spin until the tires jumped off the pavement and dug into the loose soil along the shoulder. The front end continued the spin until the vehicle came to a stop in the forest about twenty feet off the road.

. . . .

The engine whined and the truck lunged ahead again.

"Wow! Are you two okay?" Jordan said. Adrenaline-fueled excitement laced his voice.

"That was nuts," Trevor snapped.

"Woo-hoo!" Jordan laughed. "Yeah, it was, and it worked. They're toast."

Missy rubbed her neck. The ache began in her head and radiated all the way down to her tailbone. "Please. Stop. I want to get out. You can't keep me against my will."

Trevor's face pressed against her ear again. When he spoke, anger sharpened his voice with a hatred she never would have imagined he possessed. "You're with us now. You're mine."

Chapter 12

After checking to make sure Belle was okay—she was—and that the SUV was still functional—it was, barely—Andy straightened it out and headed back on the road in the direction the pickup had gone. But by the time he crested the next rise, he had lost view of the truck. Missy was gone. Again. He'd lost her. Again.

Andy hit the steering wheel and cursed under his breath. He allowed the SUV to slow to the speed limit.

"You going after her?" Belle asked.

"I'm thinking."

"Thinking's not going to find her."

He glanced at Belle. "You have a better idea?"

"Yeah. Find her."

"Easy to say."

"Hard to do. Do you let hard stop you?"

This girl made too much sense for Andy to ignore her. He pushed the gas pedal closer to the floor, and the SUV accelerated. About a mile up the road, in the middle of a heavily wooded stretch, a secondary road branched off to the right. Andy slowed the Ford again until it came to a stop in the middle of the pavement just before the turn-off.

"Which way?" Belle said.

Andy surveyed his surroundings. The road ahead wound to the left and disappeared into the forest. The road to the right branched at a forty-five-degree angle and cut a straight path through a thick patch of skeletal, leafless trees. The road was narrow, the pavement faded and crumbling in spots.

What would Trevor do? Or how about the new guy, Jordan? Which way would they take?

"'I shall be telling this with a sigh,'" Belle said, "'somewhere ages and ages hence.'"

Andy turned toward the girl. Her eyes fixated on the road to the right.

"'Two roads diverged in a wood,'" she continued, "'and I took the one less traveled by.'" She turned to look at Andy. "'And that has made all the difference.'"

Andy stared at her blankly.

"Robert Frost?"

Andy shook his head. "Nope."

"Really? So no Han Solo, no Woody Pride, no Robert Frost, but you know who Belle is. The Disney princess." She smiled. "You are one puzzling dude."

"Am I?" He motioned toward both options. "So what's your guess here?"

"No guess. Frost is the man. Take the road less traveled."

He didn't know how, but she was right. This girl had not accompanied him by accident. This was not a chance meeting. She was right; he was thankful he'd brought her along.

He turned off the main road and knew he'd made the right decision.

·······

Missy was asleep. They'd been driving for hours when she finally fell asleep, her head on his shoulder. She'd cried a lot, and he should have felt bad about that, but he didn't. He was going to kill her. There'd be a lot more crying then.

Trevor looked at the driver. Jordan. A punk. Never took anything seriously. Lived life one day at a time. He'd had contact with Jordan several times over the years, and each time he liked him more and more. He was a useful idiot. Always ready for an adventure.

Well, this would be an adventure.

Up ahead, there was an abandoned house. The occupants had left eight years ago. They'd tried to live on their own, but sickness overcame them, and one by one they'd dropped off. Nobody cared either. They were useless idiots like most people. Like Jordan.

Trevor lifted a hand and touched Missy's hair. He should kill her now, then kill the idiot. But he wanted to have some fun with her first. What was the point of having such a beauty in your possession if you couldn't enjoy her, right?

He knew who she was. Who she really was. That should scare him but it didn't. He could handle her.

The idiot glanced at him, then at the girl. "What're you gonna do with her?"

Trevor smiled. "You'll see." He motioned to the road ahead. "A couple miles farther, you'll turn left onto a gravel road. Take it to the end. There's a house. We'll spend the night there."

As he predicted, there was a house. Surprisingly, all the windows were still intact. When Jordan stopped the truck, Missy stirred.

Trevor stroked her hair. "Hey, we're here."

Missy righted herself. "Where?"

"A house. We're going to spend the night here."

Missy trembled slightly, more like a gentle vibration. "Where are we?"

Jordan said, "Somewhere in northern PA."

"We're still headed north?"

"We are," Trevor said. "All the way to Maine. Isn't that where you want to go?"

Missy didn't answer him.

"C'mon." Trevor took her hand and helped her out of the

truck. "Careful. Lots of fallen branches around here."

He led her through a maze of forest debris to the front door of the house.

"Where are we exactly?" Missy asked.

"In the woods," Trevor said. "An abandoned home. It's not the Hilton but it's shelter. It'll do for tonight." He knew that by bringing her here, to an unfamiliar place littered with obstacles and pitfalls, she wouldn't try to escape. Far too dangerous for her.

The front door of the home was still locked. Nobody came this way. Nobody cared.

"Stand back." Trevor launched himself at the door and planted his foot just to the right of the doorknob. The brittle wood splintered and broke. The door swung open.

"Awesome," Jordan said. He entered first. "Hey, there's still furniture. It stinks in here."

It did stink. People may not have cared enough about the house to occupy or destroy it, but rodents had taken a liking to it.

Trevor walked Missy to the sofa, but it was covered in mouse droppings. He reached in his bag and pulled out a folded blanket. Next to the sofa was a chair. "Jordan, clean that off, will you?"

"Sure, man." Jordan lifted the chair's cushion and brushed it off. Dust rose in a cloud. Missy coughed. "Sorry, dude," Jordan said. He replaced the cushion.

Trevor spread the blanket over the chair. "Here." He took Missy's hand and led her to the chair. "Sit."

Missy sat and kept her arms crossed over her chest. She was trying to make herself as small as possible. He'd seen frightened people do it a million times.

"What are you going to do with me, Trevor?"

Trevor didn't answer.

"Why are you keeping me against my will? I trusted you. I befriended you. I talked Andy into letting you come with us."

"Andy." Trevor hated that guy and would eventually destroy him as well. "Andy doesn't care about you. He never did. Andy's a loner. And a loser."

"He came after me."

Trevor leaned close to Missy's face. "And he lost you."

"He cares about me."

"No, he doesn't," Trevor hollered. "He couldn't care less about you."

Missy pulled back in the chair and wrapped herself tighter in her own embrace. "I want you to let me go."

Trevor stood up straight and laughed. "Really? Go where? We're in the middle of the forest. Where would you go, Missy? Huh? You gonna hike miles in the woods at night to get to the next house or town?"

"I've done it before."

"Not like this."

"You have no idea what I'm capable of."

Trevor leaned in again, so close their noses almost touched. "Oh, I know exactly what you're capable of." He backed up, reached into his bag, and pulled out a roll of duct tape. Tearing off a length of nine inches he slapped it across Missy's mouth, then grabbed her arms. "Jordan, hold her."

Jordan stepped forward and held Missy's hands together behind her back as she squirmed and writhed. "Hurry, man," Jordan said. "She's stronger than she looks."

"Hold her!" Trevor tore off another length of tape and wrapped it around Missy's wrists. Then he tore off another and bound her ankles.

Missy squirmed in the chair until she fell off and landed on the floor. She began to cry.

"Fine," Trevor said. "Have it your way. If you'd rather sleep on the floor, that's okay with me. But it's gonna be a long night, and, by the looks of it, lots of four-legged critters roam this floor."

Chapter 13

Andy continued driving even after the sun had dipped behind the tree line, leaving the sky streaked with shades of orange, pink, and purple. The barren trees, silhouetted against the evening sky, looked like bony hands breaking from the earth and reaching heavenward. If he was on the right track, he could not be that far behind. And now, he doubted it mattered. Trevor would most likely find somewhere to stop for the night. Andy had hours to find them. No need to rush.

There had been several more turns, and with each one, Belle had instructed him which way to go, and his inner nudges had confirmed her choice. As if he had some internal compass that had shifted its course. Rather than pulling him north and east, Missy was now his north star. He felt pulled to her by that same unseen magnetic force. He would not stop until he found her.

"Are you getting tired?" he asked Belle.

"Nope. Just bored."

They'd said little to each other since recovering from the accident. Andy had been lost in thought about the dreams he'd been having. They were dreams, he was sure of that, but there was more to them than a random conglomeration of memories and images. There was a purpose to them. His subconscious was trying to tell him something.

"What do you want to talk about?"

"The Event."

"Oh. You don't know about it?

"I was three when it happened."

"And no one ever told you about it?"

Belle shrugged. "Sure. Bits and pieces. I get fragments from one person, then another. But no one has ever told me the whole story. How it all started. How it ended. How it happened." She paused and glanced out the window. "Why it happened."

Andy remembered. He was fifteen when it happened. He and his mom lived in Boone, North Carolina. They'd done a good job of making it on their own. Until The Event. Then everything fell apart.

"You mind telling me about it?" Belle looked at Andy with rounded, hopeful eyes.

The girl had lost her parents during that awful time as well. She deserved to know what had happened. But Andy wouldn't have all the answers she sought. No one had all the answers.

"Sure." He drew in a deep breath. "It started with The Taking."

"Millions disappeared."

"Yeah, millions, all over the world." He snapped his fingers. "Just like that. Gone. Chaos. Plane crashes. Cars running off the road and into each other. People in an all-out panic. It hit America the hardest, paralyzed us. So much of our military and law enforcement was suddenly gone. Government workers. Congressmen. Mayors. Governors. The Vice President. All gone in an instant."

"Where did they go?"

"No one knows. Some thought it was only Christians at first, but plenty of Christians were left behind. Like my mom. She was a good woman. If only Christians were taken, she deserved to go. But she was left."

"My parents were good people," Belle said. "Christians, I guess. They took me to Sunday school and all. Told me Bible stories. Even at three, I didn't want to hear it. I wasn't interested. What do you think happened to them?"

Andy shrugged. "Many thought aliens took them. Scientists

went on and on about proof of extraterrestrials. No other plausible explanation. Some thought it was some sort of grand-scale evolutionary jump, a cleansing, they called it."

"But what do you think?"

She was pressing him for an answer, but he didn't have one. He'd thought often about it, especially right after The Taking, but he couldn't come up with a rational explanation. He didn't know. It made some sense but . . . didn't. He couldn't bring himself to believe aliens were responsible for the abduction of millions, and he had an even harder time believing the cleansing theory. "Honestly? I don't know. I've stopped thinking about it, stopped trying to figure it out."

That seemed to satisfy her. They sat in silence for a few more minutes.

"What about the animals?" she finally asked.

"Yeah, the animals. My mom said once that God gave man dominion over the earth, over the animals, but when The Event happened, and all those people disappeared, it was as if a switch was flipped in the universe and man no longer ruled. The animals rebelled. Millions of people across the world were killed."

"I heard the animals took sides, that it was divided between predator and prey."

Andy nodded. "Mostly. Predators turned against man; the prey joined us. Domestic animals went either way. It happened so fast and was so unexpected . . . there was so much confusion about why so many disappeared and why the animals suddenly revolted . . . so many died before we even figured out what was going on. I . . ." A memory long buried suddenly surfaced. "An hour or so after it happened, right after they announced it on the news, I went next door to our neighbors', Joan and Ed. They had a Sheltie named Molly. Joan and Ed were gone. Taken. And Molly . . . she came after me with such fury and hatred. Like she had some kind of personal vendetta against me, like she blamed me for the disappearance of her owners." He looked at Belle; tears streamed down her cheeks and glistened in the muted light of late evening.

"You okay?" he said.

She nodded and wiped at the tears with the back of her hand.

"You want me to stop?"

Belle shook her head. "No. I'm okay. Keep going."

"The whole thing escalated to crisis level within a few days. The National Guard, what was left of them, was dispatched, but even they were no match for the onslaught of animals and the confusion and terror that reigned everywhere. The animals outnumbered us. Some thought it was the end of the world. The apocalypse. The end of mankind. We took to hiding. Some fled to the mountains, but they didn't last long. The animals were everywhere. Most people barricaded themselves in homes or buildings. But even then, so many were killed. The animals still got to them. It seemed all was lost."

"Where did you hide?"

Another memory bobbed to the surface. "In the basement of our home with my mom. We hid down there a full month before they found us."

"Who?"

Ahead lay a fork in the road. Andy felt the pull to go left. He turned to look at Belle. "Left," she said.

"The rats," Andy said. "They chewed through the basement door. I fought them off, but there were too many of them. There was only one way to get rid of them."

He paused as his mind went back to that time.

"How?" Belle asked. She'd turned in her seat and now faced Andy.

"Fire."

His dreams. His mom. "I lit the place up. I thought my mom and I could get out, and the rats would be stuck in there, that they'd burn with the house." Tears filled his eyes and blurred the road ahead. A lump settled in his throat.

"You don't have to say anymore if you don't want to." Belle was a sensitive kid.

Andy smeared tears across his cheek. "It's okay." He swallowed hard. "Before we could get out, they got my mom. Swarmed her. I tried to free her, to get them off her, but there were too many, and the flames spread so quickly."

"That's how you got the scars."

"That's how I became a freak."

Belle reached across the seat and touched Andy's arm. "You're not a freak."

Andy ran a hand across his eyes. "The animals would have exterminated everyone if they'd had more time. But as quickly as their rampage started, it stopped, and everything went back to normal. Or at least what normal could be."

"Humans were once again in charge."

"It seemed . . . minus millions."

By now, the sun had fully set, and the sky had faded to charcoal gray. The SUV's headlights lit up the road with a wide swath of light. Ahead lay a gravel road to the right. Andy felt the pull again.

"This is it," he said as he slowed the vehicle.

Belle nodded. "Go right and you'll find Missy."

Chapter 14

Trevor sensed Andy's arrival. He stood at the front window of the house and looked out into the dark woods. The nerves running along the length of his body tingled with the anticipation of a confrontation. The freak was near.

He crossed the house to the kitchen where Jordan fiddled with a wood stove. "Hey," Trevor said.

Jordan looked up. He had soot smeared across his forehead.

"I have something I need you to do."

"Yeah? What's that?"

"Come outside with me."

Trevor led the way out the back of the house and into the clearing. He needed Jordan to deliver a message to the freak, a warning of sorts.

When they were both outside, Trevor turned and smiled at Jordan.

"What's up?" Jordan said. "What's with the goofy grin?"

Trevor launched himself at Jordan.

． ． ． ． ． ． ．

Andy parked the SUV in the middle of the gravel road. He didn't want to give Trevor and Jordan an easy escape route. He shut off the engine and killed the lights. "We hike it from here."

Belle climbed down from her seat and met Andy at the front of the vehicle. She carried a small flashlight in her hand. "It was in the glove box." She flicked it on and aimed the beam at the ground. "Still works."

"No lights," Andy said. "Keep it in your pocket, though. I'll let you know when we need it."

Belle slipped the flashlight into her pocket. "I can do stealth. That's cool."

Andy faced her until she looked up at him. "Listen, if things get rough, I want you out of the way, got it? I don't expect them to hand Missy over without a fight."

"That is, if she's even being held against her will."

Andy glanced down the gravel road. By the dusty light of the moon, he could see it stretched a little over a hundred yards before it disappeared around a bend. "She is. That stunt back there was Trevor's doing, not hers."

"So this is a rescue mission."

"Something like that." It would be much more than that, though. Andy felt the impending confrontation looming like a storm creeping over the horizon. He'd thought about leaving Belle in the SUV, but she'd be too vulnerable there. She was safest when she was with him, close by. But he'd make sure she stayed out of the fray when things got hot. "Just do as I say, okay?"

She said nothing.

"Okay?"

"Yeah, sure."

"Belle, I want you safe. You and Missy. That's it. That's my end game here. Get the two of you out of here safely."

She nodded. "I got it, Andy. I do."

"Good."

They turned and made their way down the lane, gravel crunching beneath their feet. Andy knew Trevor and Jordan would see them coming. The barren woods offered no place to hide or find cover. But he was okay with that. No use delaying the confrontation. And the element of surprise was not an option.

About a hundred yards ahead, the lane curved to the right at almost a ninety-degree angle. Around the bend and another twenty yards away, Andy saw Jordan kneeling in the middle of the lane. His face was swollen and distorted and streaked with dark red blood. The front of his shirt was soaked the same color. Andy pushed Belle behind him and advanced cautiously. As he neared, he noticed Jordan's left arm bent at an odd angle, the elbow flexed the wrong way. Blood ran in rivulets down his arm and dripped from his fingertips. Andy also noticed one eye was missing, and Jordan's nose was ripped almost entirely from his face.

When he was within fifteen feet, Jordan found him with his one eye and groaned.

"Stay close to me," Andy said to Belle. He inched closer. "Did Trevor do this?"

Jordan's voice was strained and hoarse. He wheezed when he inhaled. "Go away. He's..." Jordan could hold himself up no longer and toppled forward. He lay face down on the gravel road.

Andy stepped closer, making sure Belle stayed behind him.

"Monster," Jordan said. He tried to speak again, but all he could produce was a strained gurgling sound. Finally, he said, "Go back."

"Is Missy in there?"

But Jordan was gone. The gurgling had ceased. His one eye stared blankly at the dry ground.

"C'mon," Andy said. "Stay right behind me."

Jordan had been a warning from Trevor. The violence Trevor had inflicted on Jordan, though, had surprised and sickened him.

Another hundred yards, and the lane bent again to the right. Around the corner, a two-story German-style farmhouse with faded green asbestos siding came into view.

"There," Belle said.

"Yup. Trevor."

"And Missy."

The house looked empty, abandoned. No lights, no signs of life or occupancy at all. But Andy knew Trevor was inside, and he hoped Missy was too. He made no effort to sneak to the house or approach under cover. The sky had darkened enough that he and Belle would not be visible until they were within twenty or thirty yards. He would like to know where Missy was, though.

When they were twenty yards out, Andy stopped and raised his voice. "I got your message."

"Good." Trevor's voice floated to them from inside the house.

Andy searched the windows but saw no sign of Trevor.

"But I see you didn't take it seriously," Trevor said.

"Send Missy out and we'll leave."

"You know I can't do that."

"Why not?"

"She's something special, right? This is all about her."

Those words. The same words the old guy at the diner said to him. Andy walked closer to the house. A few feet from the front porch, he stopped. "Send her out. I don't want a fight."

Trevor chuckled. "I suspect not. You're not the violent type, right?"

He was toying with Andy. Somehow he knew of Andy's past, of his struggle. He knew of the battle that raged within him.

"Let her go, Trevor."

"You want her?" His voice had changed, deepened, become more sinister. "You'll have to come and get her."

Missy let out a muffled scream, then a moan.

Andy rushed onto the porch, Belle right behind him, and stood in front of the closed door.

"Come on in," Trevor said. "The water's great."

Andy turned to Belle and whispered, "When we get inside, I want you to stay close to the wall. When you see the chance, free Missy and get out of the house, run back to the SUV, and drive it down the lane." He gripped her shoulder. He was putting her in danger and he hated it. But it was the only way. He would occupy Trevor and keep him away from Belle and Missy. "Can you do that?"

She nodded. No fear flickered in her eyes. Only resolve and courage. "I'm Belle, remember? She took on the beast and won him over."

"Good girl. Drive to the end of the lane. I'll catch up. But if I don't, and if Trevor comes out of the house instead of me, just drive, and don't stop until you're safe."

She nodded again.

Andy straightened, tensed his muscles, and opened the door.

Chapter 15

Trevor met him on the other side of the door in an abrupt and violent reception fueled by hatred and malice of the foulest order. He charged Andy and pinned him against the wall. The force of his attack knocked the air from Andy's lungs. Andy gasped and momentarily lost focus of the smaller man. But in the corner of his vision, he saw Belle rush to the other side of the room. Hopefully, Missy was there.

Trevor said nothing. Instead, he delivered a fisted blow to Andy's stomach that again forced air from his lungs and sent nausea radiating from his abdomen all the way to his throat. He thought he'd vomit. Blow after blow, the assault came. Trevor's tremendous strength and quickness were surprising. Finally, he lifted Andy from his feet and launched him across the room with no more effort than he'd toss a doll into the garbage.

Andy struck the wall with incredible force, rattling it all the way from the foundation to the ceiling. Somehow he remained on his feet and recovered enough to meet Trevor's next advance with an attack of his own. As Trevor charged, grunting like a wild animal, Andy stepped forward and landed a punch to the smaller man's chest that would have killed an ordinary man. Rage exploded within Andy, the kind of rage that frightened him, the rage that he fought to contain. But this was no time to control it. He allowed the rage to overcome him, to shake loose its restraints and have its way.

The blow had pushed Trevor back a few steps, but it failed to knock him down and failed to incapacitate him even for a moment. Trevor shook it off as if it were a pat on the back and advanced again. He narrowed his eyes and gritted his teeth. He seethed and grunted. Connected with Andy with such forward momentum that it pushed both of them into the wall. The plaster broke and crumbled; studs cracked. The house shuddered. Pain shot through Andy's back like a lightning bolt. But he fed on the pain now, allowed it to fuel his hot rage. Driving his head into Trevor's chest, he pushed the shorter man backward until they met the other wall. Trevor exhaled sharply; Andy took advantage of the moment. He landed a punch to Trevor's stomach, then another and another. Alternating right and left hands, he delivered a series of punches as rapidly as machine-gun fire.

Finally, he grabbed Trevor by the neck and squeezed. He wanted to crush the smaller man's trachea and smother what life was left.

· · · · · · ·

The moment the door opened and the fight began, Missy's stomach curled into a knot. Trevor was not who she had thought he was. She had been duped. Tears flowed from her eyes. And now Andy had to confront the consequence of her misjudgment. He never wanted to pick up Trevor; he didn't want Missy hanging out with Trevor. But she'd ignored him and it had come to this.

Trevor was evil. She felt it, experienced it. Confronted it in her own way.

Until the girl arrived at her side and ripped at the tape that bound Missy's wrists and ankles, she thought Andy had come alone. Jordan was gone. And she wondered if Andy would be able to withstand the monster that was Trevor.

The girl said her name was Belle. She assured Missy that she was with Andy, and they were there to rescue her. Once the tape had been removed, both Missy and Belle scrambled back to the wall, hoping to stay out of the fight.

The fight. Such violence. Wood cracked, and the house groaned under the weight and impact of bodies colliding. Andy and Trevor battered each other. The house's aging foundation quaked and creaked.

Missy reached for the girl, Belle, and held her close. In the darkness, Missy sought the light, that light that was always there, leading her, guiding her, protecting her.

Where was the light?

. . . .

Trevor still had plenty of fight in him. The man's stamina and strength were unbelievable. Inhuman. Trevor managed to break free from Andy's grip and kneed him in the groin. He landed a blow to Andy's side, his chest, then his neck. With each hit, the force increased. The man didn't tire; his muscles refused to fatigue. His strength was . . . otherworldly.

Andy slumped to the floor where Trevor kicked him, landing shots to the abdomen and chest, one to Andy's face. Andy curled into a tight ball and hoped the assault would soon end.

And it did. Trevor paused but only long enough to grip Andy by his shirt and pants, lift him as if he were a small child, and launch him against the ceiling. Andy hit it with such force he thought he'd broken the support beams and the entire second floor would collapse upon them. He hit the hardwood flooring face down and lay stunned.

It was too much. Trevor's strength and quickness had proved to be more than Andy could defend against, let alone overcome. The man was not of this world. No human could do what he did.

Trevor sat on Andy's back and pinned him to the floor. "I'm going to kill you." His voice was deep and raspy, not Trevor's voice. This man may look like Trevor, but he was not Trevor at all.

He gripped beneath Andy's chin with both hands and pulled

upward, forcing Andy's neck into such extreme extension it nearly cracked. Andy fought back, strained against the pressure, but the Trevor-thing's strength was too much.

Across the room, Andy found Belle and Missy huddled against the wall. Both appeared to be unharmed.

Missy scooted forward on the floor. "Stop it, Trevor. You're killing him."

"I'm going to kill him, then I'm gonna kill you," Trevor said. He pulled harder on Andy's neck. No way Andy's spine could take much more. Eventually, his muscles would fatigue, and the bones would crack as if they were made of balsa wood.

"Stop it!" Missy cried. She got to her hands and knees, then just her knees. Sobs racked her body. "Stop. Please."

Trevor continued to pull. Andy grunted and strained against the pressure. He couldn't resist much longer.

"No!" Missy inched closer as her body began to convulse like a dog writhes right before it vomits.

Missy groaned and clenched her teeth. Every muscle in her body tensed and contracted. Tighter and tighter until she was as rigid as a concrete beam.

Andy thought she was having some sort of seizure—until the fire came.

Chapter 16

The fire. If he hadn't seen it with his own eyes, if he hadn't felt the scorching heat on his own skin, and if he hadn't witnessed Trevor stumbling around the house like a rag doll on fire, he wouldn't have believed it.

Missy had convulsed, opened her mouth, and spit fire like a flamethrower. The jet of flames missed Andy's head and hit Trevor square in the face and chest. Trevor fell from Andy's back and writhed on the floor until he managed to climb to his feet. His head and upper torso were engulfed in flames as he lurched and staggered around the room, flailing his arms and clawing at the flames that spread down his body. Finally, he crashed into the wall and fell limp. The flames then spread from Trevor to the brittle, crumbling plaster. They climbed the wall and lapped at the ceiling.

"C'mon," Andy hollered. "Everyone out."

Missy had collapsed after heaving the fire and only now stirred. Andy lifted her into his arms and hurried out of the house, making sure Belle was in front of him and always in his view.

They ran until they were a safe distance from the house; then all three fell to the forest floor, panting and sweating.

Missy was still delirious. "What happened?"

Andy looked from her to the house, then back to her. "You don't know?"

Missy held her head in her hands. "My head is killing me."

Trevor appeared in the doorway of the house. Flames leaped from his charred body. The house around him was an inferno, throwing fire ten, twenty feet into the evening sky. But Trevor was not done. He stumbled onto the porch, then down the steps, his legs moving like they were made of rubber, his arms windmilling wildly. He made it another fifteen feet off the porch and collapsed face first onto the ground.

"We gotta get out of here," Andy said. He lifted Missy to her feet. "Can you walk?"

She nodded. "Yeah. I think so."

Andy found Belle standing behind him, staring at Trevor's burning corpse. He turned her head away from it. "C'mon kid, let's go."

When they arrived at the SUV, Andy made sure Missy was safely buckled into the passenger seat. Belle took the back seat.

He brought the engine to life, backed out of the lane, turned onto the road, and headed north.

For a few minutes, nothing but the sound of their heavy breathing filled the cabin of the SUV. Andy's pulse thumped in his ears and the whole way down to his fingertips. Beside him, Missy wrapped herself in a tight hug.

Finally, Belle said, "Are we gonna talk about what happened back there?"

"What happened?" Missy asked.

"Uh, you totally dragon-spit fire at that dude."

Missy stared straight ahead. "I don't remember."

Belle tapped Andy on the shoulder. "And how are you not dead after the beating he gave you? He tossed you against the ceiling like you were a stuffed animal." She sat back hard in the seat. "What's happening?"

"How did you do that?" Andy asked Missy.

She shook her head. "I don't know. I don't remember doing it. I remember the fight and Trevor . . . the darkness." She put both hands to her head. "The darkness was suffocating. I was so scared. I thought he was going to kill you. Then . . . that's it. I came to and the house was on fire."

"Yeah," Belle said. "You did that. You lit that dude up. How is that even possible?"

Missy stared at Andy.

"What?" he said.

"You came after me."

"I wasn't going to let him take you away."

She reached across the center console and placed her hand over his. "Thank you."

"Hello?" Belle leaned forward again. "Are we just going to ignore the fact that one of you is indestructible and the other projectile vomits fire?"

"How did you do that?" Missy asked Andy.

"I don't know. I've always been different like that."

"Different? Is that what you call it?" Belle said.

"Different. My mom told me I had to control it, bring it into submission, hide it from the world. I've tried."

"So it's real," Belle said. "It wasn't our imagination that you took the beating of your life and walked away from it."

"I gave a beating too, didn't I?"

"Yeah, and that dude was like you. Only badder."

He was badder. How did Trevor withstand the violence that Andy had unleashed on him? A normal man would have been killed. Was Trevor like him? Different? Were there others out there like him?

Outside the SUV, moonlight filtered through the trees and cast the forest in a muted, gloomy light. The road emerged from the forest and sloped upward toward a ridge.

"The fire," Missy said. "Was it real?"

She was still in disbelief. She had no idea what she was capable of. She'd unleashed it on the punks yesterday and now on Trevor. Andy didn't know how it was possible, but it had happened. He hadn't imagined it. The house and Trevor's corpse were proof. "Yes. It was real."

"Great," Belle said. She sat back hard in the seat again. "I'm hangin' out with the X-Men."

Chapter 17

A couple hours later, they stopped at a bar near the Pennsylvania–New York line. The place was dark and musty; a thin film of smoke clung to the ceiling. A bar lined one wall, backless stools pushed up under it. A few lonely men sat there, nursing whatever brought them comfort. Tables and chairs and only a few patrons occupied the rest of the main eating area. A middle-aged couple sat at one table. Andy eyed their plates of food, and his stomach growled in anticipation. He hadn't eaten since yesterday. Neither had Missy or Belle. They all needed some grub in their bellies.

Booths lined the perimeter of the bar. They took a seat and quickly ordered sandwiches and drinks from a young waitress named Albany.

They took turns using the bathroom while they waited for the food. When it came, they dug in, saying little to each other. Hunger has a funny way of taking priority over conversation.

·······

They were in the bar like he knew they would be. The old man sat with his back to the threesome. He needed to keep an eye on them, but that was all. He was not to interfere. Not yet. Not here. They needed to navigate their own way for now. All part of the process for the girl. She needed to grow and discover what she was truly capable of. And true learning could only come from doing, exploring, discovering. From experience.

The man had seen others walk the same road the girl was on. It was full of potholes and obstacles and pitfalls. There would be failures and triumphs, discouragement and victories. So many others had trod the same path and experienced the same valleys and mountains. And he'd watched them all, helped some. He would allow her to fail, but she would eventually succeed. It had been ordained. He counted himself fortunate to have a front-row seat to watch her blossom. She was so important, so critical to the path humanity must take. And she had no idea. Not yet.

But she would discover her purpose soon enough.

•••••••

When all the plates were clear and all hunger satisfied, Belle said, "Seriously, guys, can we talk about what happened back at the house?"

Andy knew they had to talk about it sooner or later. Really talk about it. He was as floored by Missy's ability as Belle was. And even Missy seemed baffled by it. "Sure. What do you want to talk about?"

Belle leaned her elbows on the table and shifted her eyes between Andy and Missy. "Uh, fire-breathing women and indestructible men?"

"I can't breathe fire," Missy said.

"And I'm not indestructible," Andy added.

Belle grabbed a sugar packet. "Close enough." She turned to Missy. "How does it work?"

"I don't know."

"Where does it come from?"

"I don't know."

"Can you control it?"

"I don't know."

Belle spun the sugar packet on the table. "Okay, well, that clears things up."

Missy sipped her soda, then said, "Look, up until yesterday, I didn't even know I could do that. I didn't know I had the . . . ability. I don't remember anything about it, honestly. Both times I got this feeling like I was going to vomit, only way more intense, then nothing. I must black out. When I come to, I have this splitting headache, and my mouth feels like it's on fire."

"I guess it does," Belle said.

"It's like it's involuntary."

"But how is it even physically possible?"

Missy shrugged. "I don't know."

While Missy spoke, Andy glanced around the bar. The couple at the table had glanced their way several times. They were talking about the threesome, or at least about Andy. Maybe they'd noticed his face. Maybe it was . . . something else. After both encounters with Colin and the other punks yesterday and Trevor today, he was jittery about the attention of strangers. The men at the bar mostly ignored them. One of them, a scruffy young guy with a patchy beard and glassy eyes, turned and stared hard at Missy and Belle for a few seconds, but other than that, the bar-sitters appeared uninterested.

Andy turned his attention back to the conversation. "It's not physically possible. We recognize that there's something else in play here."

"This is like the X-Files," Belle said.

Andy and Missy stared blankly at her.

"Oh, come on. Seriously? Mulder and Scully?" Belle shook her head.

The blank looks lingered.

"And what about you?" Missy said to Andy.

"I told you. I'm different."

"How?"

He motioned to Belle. "According to her, I'm indestructible. Haven't you noticed? I'm like a superhero."

"But why. How did that happen?"

Andy hadn't told his companions his entire story. He wasn't sure he wanted to tell them. "My father was like me, only more so."

"Was your father Thor?" Belle asked.

When Andy ignored her question, she said, "What was he like?"

"I don't know. He died before I was born. My mom didn't talk about him much, only that she was glad he was gone. He was different too . . . but in a different way than me."

Missy shifted in her seat. "Different how?"

Andy shrugged. The conversation made him uncomfortable. He was his father's son and yet he wasn't. He didn't want to be like his father. "Apparently, he embraced his differentness. Used it to do some very bad things. Hurt people."

"Including your mother?" Missy knew the type all too well. From what she'd told him so far, she'd endured more than he ever had.

"Yes. Even my mother."

"How did he die?"

"I don't know. My mom would never go that far in the conversation. She'd change the subject before it got to that point."

Belle leaned closer. "Was your dad a mutant like you?"

Andy stared at her for a few seconds. "I'm not a mutant."

"Then what are you? No one has strength like that. Except maybe Wolverine."

"Who?"

"Never mind. So you're different than your dad but not that different. Just different in a different sort of way."

Again, Andy stared at her. "I'm beginning to wonder why I brought you along."

Belle sat back in the booth and spun the sugar packet. "You two are full of enlightening information." She nodded her head toward Missy. "You have no idea about anything." Then to Andy. "And all you know is that your dad was different but in a different way than you're different."

Missy turned her face to Belle. "And who are you? Where did you come from?" She looked in Andy's direction. "Why is she even here?"

After a brief awkward silence, Andy said, "She helped me find you. I couldn't have done it without her." It was the truth too.

Belle continued to spin the sugar packet. Andy put his hand over it to stop the spinning. "How did you know?"

"Know what?"

"Where to turn. Where the house would be."

Belle shrugged. "I don't know. I just felt it."

"Like a magnetic pull?"

"Yeah, something like that. I sense things."

Andy smiled. "Like a mutant?"

"What kinds of things?" Missy asked.

"Things. About people, places. Just feelings."

"Like?"

"Like what kind of people they are, what kind of place it is. When I saw you talking in the gym last night, I knew right away that those two dudes were no good. I knew they were up to something. So I kept my eye on them. Then when you"—she pointed to Andy—"woke up this morning, I knew I needed to help you. I was the only one who could."

"So you're different too." Andy smirked. "But a different kind of different than our different."

"I guess," she said. "You're like superheroes or mutants or something. I'm not like that. I can't breathe fire, and my bones aren't made of iron."

"But you see people," Missy said.

"But not dead people."

"No. You see them for who they really are."

"What about the folks in this bar?" Andy glanced at the other patrons. "Anyone catch your attention?"

"Yeah, creepy dude over there on the stool. If you weren't here, big guy, he'd have made a move on us already. He's a creeper, for sure."

Just then an older man sitting at the bar stood, put a few bills on the counter, and walked toward the door. As he passed the creepy guy, he turned and glanced in the direction of the threesome's table.

When Andy's eyes met the older man's, a chill raced down Andy's spine. There was a familiarity about him that immediately gnawed at Andy's mind. Where did he know him from?

"Wait here," Andy said. He slid out of the booth as the old guy exited the building. Dashing through the room, Andy wove around tables and reached the door in a matter of seconds. He pushed open the door in time to catch the mystery man getting into his truck, a late-model Dodge.

The man fired up the engine, but Andy got there before he could step on the gas. Andy positioned himself in front of the truck, both hands on the hood, and stared at the man. He knew this guy. Somehow and from somewhere, but he couldn't place him.

The man stared back. He couldn't have been more than sixty, but age had not been kind to him. He'd lived a hard life, weathered many storms.

"Who are you?" Andy asked.

The man said nothing. He shifted the truck into gear.

"I'm not moving until you tell me."

The man rolled the driver's side window down. "I'll run you over."

"No, you won't. You know you can't. Who are you? How did you know we'd be here?"

After a few tense beats, the man relaxed behind the wheel. "I was a friend of your mother's."

"What's your name?"

"Names aren't important."

Andy recalled his mother talking about a Ben Baxter, the pastor of the church she attended as a teen.

"Ben Baxter."

The man said nothing.

"Are you Ben Baxter?"

The man looked like he wanted to say something, like he had confidential information he was itching to share but couldn't. He tightened his lips and looked around the empty parking lot. "No. I can't say anything more. Not yet. You're going to have to figure this out on your own. That's the way it has to be. Now please, let me go."

"But you knew we'd be here. At this bar on this day."

Again, the man responded with silence.

"I'm not moving until you tell me how you knew we'd be here."

"I just knew. I needed to make sure you both were okay."

"How did you know?"

"He told me."

"Who?"

The man pointed a finger heavenward. "You better get back inside. Your companions are gonna need you."

Andy stared at him, debating whether to let him go or not.

"Scruffy at the bar's been eyeing them up since you all walked in."

The creeper.

"Will we see you again?" Andy asked.

The old man smiled. Some of his teeth were missing, but it was a nice smile that wrinkled his eyes at the corners. "I hope so. Get to Boston. I'll meet you there, and when the time is right, I'll tell you what you need to know. I can't talk now. Not here. Not now." He nodded toward to the bar. "Now go. They need you. Now."

Andy lifted his hands from the truck's hood and stepped to the side. The man drove by without another look at Andy.

Inside the bar, Andy found creeper guy at the table, leaning on it like he owned it. His face was inches from Missy's.

Andy quickly crossed the room and stood behind the guy. "Back off, dude."

The creep turned and straightened his back, stuck out his chest. The smell of alcohol clung to him like a cheap cologne. He was a full four inches shorter than Andy and probably forty pounds lighter. When he noticed Andy's face and Stetson, his mouth split into a wide smile. "Where'd they find you, the cowboy freak show?"

Anger tightened Andy's fists but he relaxed them. He didn't want to hurt this guy. He was drunk and feeling a little too sure of himself. Instead, Andy turned a quarter turn, hoping to relieve some of the tension that had built between the two by disengaging. He redirected his attention to Missy and Belle. "You two ready to go?"

"Who do you think you are, huh?" The creep didn't know when to walk away.

Andy turned back to face the guy. "I'm the guy telling you to back off. Walk away and go back to your beer."

"Man, I'm not going anywhere unless I have one of these young ladies on my arm."

"Then it'll be a broken arm," Andy said.

From across the room, the bartender said, "Hey, guys, you got issues, take 'em outside."

"We were just leaving," Andy said. He stepped forward into the creep's space to force him away from the booth so Missy and Belle could exit.

But creepy-guy didn't like being maneuvered. He tried to hold his ground, but Andy was too big and bulky for him to stop. Instead, he dug in his heels, shifted his weight forward, and tried to head-butt Andy in the jaw. Andy was too quick, though, and saw the move coming. He sidestepped, caught the guy off-balance, and shoved him forward. The creep stumbled for a couple steps, his center of gravity too far out in front of him, then lost his balance and fell into another booth.

Andy turned to Missy and Belle. "Now leave. Head for the SUV. I'll be right behind you." He knew the creep wouldn't take being humiliated with a good attitude. Alcohol had a way of amping someone's pride to unhealthy levels.

By the time Missy and Belle were halfway across the room, the guy had climbed to his feet, cursing and spitting blood. He'd apparently hit his mouth on the table and busted his lip.

Andy had placed himself between the girls and the creep and backpedaled across the bar.

The creep looked around, found them near the door, cursed again, and charged Andy.

It was an unfair match. Andy knew that. He simply shoved the man, who lost his balance again and this time stumbled into a stool and knocked it over, falling on top of it.

The bartender waved Andy out of the building. "Go on. Get. I'll take care of him."

Outside, the sky was still dark, but the lot seemed darker. The one sodium bulb that illuminated the area had gone out.

The SUV waited across the lot, fifteen yards away.

Belle took Andy's arm, stopped him and Missy. "Wait."

"What is it?" Andy surveyed the lot but couldn't make much out in the darkness.

"Something's here."

"Some*thing* or some*one*?" Missy said.

"Does it matter?"

From behind the SUV came a rustling, like that of an animal caught in a thicket and trying to free itself.

Chapter 18

There's an eeriness that typically surrounds a coyote in the wild. That eeriness increases exponentially when a pack is present. What emerged from beyond the SUV was not just one coyote but five—all mangy with long, lanky legs and slender torsos. The alpha was larger and jet black, its fur longer than the others' as well.

As if they'd discussed their strategy ahead of time, the pack spread out and surrounded Andy, Missy, and Belle.

Missy must have felt Andy tense. "What is it?"

"Coyotes."

"How many?"

"Five. They're surrounding us."

The coyotes formed a perimeter around the threesome at a distance of fifteen to twenty feet. All except the alpha paced a small track—mouths closed, ears low, heads dipped—watching the humans with intense curiosity. The alpha stood his ground in a slight crouch, his yellow eyes never moving from their target. An image of Dean Shannon shot through Andy's mind. Head dipped, fists clenched, feet spread wide, arms tense and ready for action. He'd been a predator of sorts.

"Do they look friendly?" Missy asked.

Belle leaned into Andy. "They look like they want to eat us."

That same hungry look had flashed in Dean's eyes.

"Just stand still." Andy needed to think, formulate a plan to scatter the coyotes, break up the pack, and cause confusion. That would give an opening and the time needed to rush to the SUV, just twenty feet away.

The coyotes moved in synchrony, inching closer, tightening the circle to ten feet.

Dean had moved in a similar manner, circling Andy, stalking him. Eyeing his prey.

The alpha yelped, and one of the coyotes to Andy's right bared its teeth, snarled, and let out a sharp bark. It lunged forward, within five feet of Missy, then scurried back to its original position.

The one to Andy's left did the same.

"What are they doing?" Missy asked.

"Coordinating," Andy said. "Planning." Intelligent behavior, but not beyond a pack of coyotes. They hunted in packs and often coordinated their movements for the most efficient attack.

Belle leaned even closer into Andy. "I thought you said it was over."

"It is," he said. "This is different."

"Really? How?"

Andy had seen a pack of wolves behave in a similar manner shortly after The Event. He'd stood by helplessly as a family was surrounded and stalked and eventually devoured. The wolves had coordinated their movements, communicated through yelps and snarls. It had made Andy physically sick at the time, and the memory of the ordeal now stirred those nauseating feelings. "Maybe it's not so much different."

The coyotes inched closer again, wagging their heads back and forth in an irritated manner. The alpha's pink tongue darted in and out of its mouth. His crouch deepened.

Dean's taunts had stirred something in Andy, something foreign and ugly. Malicious. Something that clawed and snarled and spit and hissed. Andy's temper was no secret, nor was his unusual strength . . . but this was different. It had its source in some dark abyss buried under layers of his soul.

Missy tightened her grasp on Andy's arm. "What should we do?"

"Can't you light them up?" Belle asked.

"No," Missy said. "I can't flip it on and off with a switch. I don't know how to control it."

There were too many for Andy to take on at once. If it were just one, even the larger alpha, he might stand a chance, but not against the five. Their attacks would be relentless and would wear him down systematically until he had no more strength. And then they'd devour him.

But he had an idea. "Can you drive, Belle?"

"Sure."

"What are you thinking?" Missy asked.

"I can hold them off," Andy said. "You two make a run for it. Belle, you drive. Head north. I'll catch up with you."

His plan made no sense, and he doubted they'd go for it.

He was right.

"No way," Missy said. "You'll never make it out."

The coyotes came no closer, but they all bobbed their heads now and flicked their tongues. They were growing increasingly agitated.

"Can you take them?" Belle said.

"I can hold them off." It would be the best he could do.

"You said that the first time. Can you take them, though?"

The alpha lunged to within three feet of the threesome and snapped its jaws but quickly retreated. It yelped once, and the coyote to its left did the same.

"We need to do this now," Andy said. "On the count of three, okay?"

Neither of his companions said anything.

"Really, we need to do this," he said again. "On three make a run for the SUV."

But before he could begin counting, the door to the bar flew open, and a voice bellowed from behind them. "Yah! Get outta here!" A gunshot pierced the still night air and echoed across the vast open space surrounding the bar. One of the coyotes flinched, yelped, stumbled a few feet to its right, then slumped to the ground, motionless. The others scurried into the darkness.

"Get outta here!" the man yelled. Another crack from the gun sounded. Missy jumped.

Andy turned to find the bartender standing outside the bar, rifle pointing skyward. "Blasted coyotes. Keep comin' 'round here lookin' for food." He eyed Andy and the girls. "Looks like you were almost their food."

"It looked that way," Andy said. "Thanks for coming when you did."

The bartender crossed the parking lot to where the coyote lay. He nudged it with his foot, which produced a weak whine from the coyote. After stepping back a few feet, the bartender pointed the rifle at the coyote's head and squeezed off another round. The concussion was deafening. The coyote flinched, then lay lifeless.

Chapter 19

Belle slept in the back seat of the SUV while Andy drove and Missy entertained thoughts of gruesome, ugly images. She was tired, fatigued from a long, arduous day and night topped off by a frightening encounter with coyotes, but she could not sleep. She'd gone from running from Andy to captivity by Trevor to being rescued by Andy to facing down a pack of hungry coyotes.

Not to mention her apparent ability to spit fire. She still could not comprehend how it happened. Scientifically—biologically—it was impossible. Humans do not possess the ability to breathe fire. Her mother told her once that cows belch methane, and some people believed fire-breathing dinosaurs may have once roamed the earth. But humans? No. Not possible.

Or was it? Maybe not biologically, but she had obviously done it. She'd burned Trevor to death. She had no memory of it, but, well, there it was, the truth. She'd taken his life. She was glad she could not see his burning body, but she had smelled it, that biting odor of burning flesh.

Andy had said little the past two hours. He was intent on getting as far north as they could before daybreak. Traveling at night seemed safer, he'd said. Fewer prying eyes. They called him a freak but Missy didn't know why. He'd probably grown used to moving under cover of darkness, hiding whatever deformity he had from the world around him.

She sensed that he was a tortured man, beaten by his own guilt and self-loathing. He had no faith in himself let alone in anyone else. He needed an awakening; he needed to know how much he mattered in the greater scheme. Missy knew it. She felt it. The leading, the purpose, the love. She'd been led and protected. She'd been led to Andy. No mistake, no spin of fate's magic wheel had brought the two of them together. There was a purpose for it, a plan. Andy didn't know it yet, but there was a plan for him too, something important, something way beyond their ability to comprehend. There was a plan for her too. She felt it. But first, she had to get to Maine. She didn't know what awaited her there, but she knew it would test her to the core of her faith and courage.

Her mind then went to her mother, and she dwelt on happy thoughts—laughter and smiles and holding hands and cuddling. She focused on the image of her mother. But there was something wrong, something different about the way she saw her mother. Her face, once so beautiful, soft and kind, was now hard and angular, the skin stretched tight. Gradually, almost imperceptibly, her face changed. Her eyes deepened and cheekbones sharpened. Then, as if a light switch had been flipped and some evil light had been cast on her mother's once sweet face, it changed. This thing in her mind was no longer her mother. The teeth were rotted and sharp, the eyes narrowed and sunken, the lips stretched into thin lines, and the flesh had become taut and gray.

Missy flinched and jumped, let out a soft gasp. She wanted to close her eyes and make it go away, hide it in the darkness of her mind, but the darkness was already there.

Andy touched her leg. "Hey, you okay?"

The image vanished. "Yeah," she lied. "Just fell asleep there for a second and startled."

"What are you thinking about?"

"My mother."

"Good thoughts?"

She paused. "Mostly. What do you do when you're haunted by memories?"

Memories. They haunted him daily, constantly. Looping in and out and around in his mind like some old movie reel that wouldn't stop. His mother. The rats. The fire. Dean Shannon. Ghostly images from his past that tormented him in wakefulness and sleep. He couldn't escape them.

A memory surfaced then. Dean Shannon. The fight. Such fury. Such hatred and primal rage. Andy had allowed whatever devil resided inside him to have its way. He'd given up control. Was it Dean's fault? Andy had tried to convince himself it was. As Dean lay there clinging to life, his blood soaking into the dirt floor of the stable, his breaths ragged and uneven, Andy told the dying man he should have walked away, he should have turned his back.

"Hey." Missy's hand was on his arm.

"Yeah." She'd asked him a question about his haunting memories. "Uh, my memories. I don't do anything about them. I can't." He hesitated, gripped the steering wheel tighter. "I live with them."

Missy sat quietly for a full minute before saying, "I guess we're all haunted in some way."

"Yeah, I guess we are. Some more than others."

"Maybe we're haunted by memories because we've never given them up."

"What do you mean?"

"We cling to them." She turned a little in her seat so she faced Andy. "You know, it's like we continue to feed them. Like a stray dog you don't want around, but you keep slipping him table scraps. He keeps coming back. Maybe these memories come back because we keep feeding them."

"I'm not following. How are we feeding them?"

"Regret. Fear. Anger. They're all food for these memories. The more we hang on to the feelings that surround them, the longer the dreams hang around. Keep coming back for scraps."

She made sense. Andy had clung to those feelings and emotions. He'd kept feeding those memories. And they kept coming back for more. "You should sleep while you can. Sun'll be up soon, and then we'll stop for breakfast, okay?"

She forced a smile and nodded. "Yeah, sure."

Missy laid her head against the door and closed her eyes. The vibration of the road rattled her skull against the glass, but she welcomed the distraction. An image of her mother once again flickered in her mind, but this time it was her, not the demon-like creature.

Eventually, sleep overcame Missy, and she drifted into the sea of slumber.

·······

They were in some small town in western Massachusetts. A sign several miles back said Roxbury, but Andy wasn't sure if this was Roxbury or not. The town consisted of one intersection with a four-way stop, a diner, an operating gas station, and a handful of homes, half of which were boarded and apparently vacated long ago.

Andy steered the truck into the small, busted-up parking lot of Elva's Eat & Carry and nudged Missy. She stirred, let out a deep sigh, and opened her eyes. "Where are we?"

"Somewhere in Massachusetts. Roxbury, I think."

She righted herself in the seat and turned her face toward the windshield. "Has daybreak come?"

"Yeah, about an hour ago."

In the back seat, Belle shifted and yawned. "Hey, where are we?"

"Good morning," Missy said.

"Where are we?" A hint of irritation to her voice.

Andy turned in the seat. "Don't like mornings?"

"Where are we?"

"Massachusetts. Elva's."

"That's the name of the town? Elvis?"

"No, Elva's. The restaurant."

Belle leaned to the side so she could get a better view out the window. "Is that what you call this?"

"It has food."

"Let's hope so. And coffee. I need coffee."

"You're thirteen."

"I'm a thirteen-year-old who needs coffee."

"Well let's go see what Elva's got cooking."

The three exited the SUV and entered the diner. It was like any other small-town diner. Booths, tables, a counter with stools. The place had not aged well and was in need of an update. There were no patrons or staff in view. A handwritten sign invited guests to seat themselves.

Andy led Missy and Belle to a table near the door.

Moments later, a waitress exited the kitchen area. She couldn't have been more than fifteen or sixteen, thin as a pole and pale as goat cheese. She approached the table and stopped five feet away. Stared at Andy. "Just the three of you?"

"Yes," Missy said. She must have sensed the girl's unease at the sight of a disfigured man, a blind woman, and a young teen. None of them had showered or groomed themselves since they'd left the shelter.

The girl snapped the gum in her mouth. "What can I get for you then?"

They gave their orders, and the girl promised it would only be a few minutes.

When she left the table, Missy said, "First order of business after this is to find a place where we can shower."

"You got that right," Belle said. "You're puttin' off some pretty ripe odors there, big guy."

Andy shrugged. He'd noticed, but there was nothing to do about it.

"Campgrounds always have showers," Belle said.

"First, we find some gas, then find a shower," Andy said.

"There's got to be a campground nearby."

The meal came, and they all dug in, had their fill, drank their coffee. With her plate clear and third cup of coffee drained, Belle sat back and sighed.

"Full?" Andy sipped the last of the coffee from his own mug.

"You betcha," Belle said.

"How 'bout you, Missy?"

"Oh yes. The eggs were great." She'd ordered two eggs, over easy, and home fries. "Just what I needed." She wiped her mouth with the napkin and sipped at the hot tea she had ordered. Then she said, "Can we talk about something?"

Andy straightened in his chair. "Sure." He glanced toward the kitchen but saw no one. The entire time they'd been in the diner no one else had come through the door. He thought it strange that the place had no customers. But then again, the town probably consisted of no more than twenty people. There were outlying areas, of course, but the restaurant had no doubt been limping along for years following The Event. It had found a way to survive, though. Andy hoped it wasn't by serving outdated food.

Missy's eyes darted around Andy's face. "Do you think Trevor had been targeting us?"

"What do you mean?"

"I mean, from the time we picked him up along the side of the road, do you think he intended to kidnap me all along?"

"That dude was bad news, I'll tell you that," Belle said.

"I don't know," Andy said. He had wondered the same thing, though.

"If he did, why?" Missy said. She'd obviously been thinking about this, and it bothered her.

Andy reached across the table and placed his hand on Missy's. "It might be that he was just some guy looking for a ride at the beginning, but then he concocted that plan and found an accomplice to go along with it."

"He fooled me," Missy said, her voice dropping in volume.

The thought of being duped by such a cruel, evil person noticeably bothered her.

"Not me," Belle said. "Dude was evil from the get-go. I mean, like, Hannibal Lecter evil."

"Who's that?" Andy said.

Belle rolled her eyes. "Never mind."

Missy finished her tea. "I get the feeling he wasn't some loner gone rogue."

"What do you mean?"

She sighed. "I don't know. I feel something coming, like Colin and Trevor are part of something bigger—two actors, different scenes, but same play."

Andy looked to Belle. "What do you think?"

She held up both hands. "Don't look at me. I'm not a big-picture girl. I can mark the creeps, but forget it when it comes to plans."

"Well, regardless," Andy said, "I think we need to be extra cautious, watch each other's backs."

Missy smiled. "We're a team."

"Like the X-Men," Belle said.

"Now let's get outta here." Andy stood and placed a few bills on the table. "We need gas and showers."

· · · · · · ·

Outside the diner, the man watched from across the street as the SUV drove away from the restaurant. He knew they were headed toward the campground, and he knew they'd find overpriced gas at the Mobil station just outside of town. He knew it because the voices told him so. And the voices never lied. They were never wrong.

When the SUV was out of sight, he got in his own truck, started the engine, and headed northwest. Toward the Stay N Play RV Campground.

Chapter 20

The shower was cold as ice. When they'd pulled into the campground, only three algae-covered campers were parked in lots. The campground had long ago turned off the utilities. The bathrooms were no doubt fed by a well, and someone had left the electricity running to the pumps so water could be available. That was kind of them. Unfortunately, that same electricity didn't power the water heaters, and no one had bothered to connect the lines.

Although the water was frigid, the shower still felt good. It had been days since Andy had bathed in any way, and getting the grime and sweat off his body was worth enduring the cold water.

The girls waited outside in the SUV. Andy had placed Belle behind the wheel and given them strict instructions to keep the doors locked; if anything went bad, she was to floor it to the next town north. He'd catch up with them. If all went well, they were to shower after him while he kept watch.

Sticking his head under the water, the coldness momentarily took his breath away. When he closed his eyes and held his breath, he was met with an image of violence and gore. Dean Shannon's mangled, bloody body. So much blood. Andy pulled his head from the shower spray, wiped the water from his face, and opened his eyes. Was that a noise outside the bathroom? A thud—like something large dropped or a car door slammed shut.

Andy shut off the water and stood there naked, listening, shivering. He had no towel, and the paper towel dispenser was empty. He'd have to air dry.

There, he heard it again, this time clearly and loud. A thud. Definitely the sound of a car door shutting. The sound was followed by a shriek. Missy.

Andy stepped from the shower and, still dripping wet, pulled his clothes on as quickly as possible. He rushed from the bathroom to find the building surrounded by pickups and SUVs. Five of them.

In the middle of the clearing around the bathroom stood six men of varying ages and builds. And in the middle of the men stood Missy and Belle. Belle's shirt was torn, and she had to hold her hand over her chest to avoid being exposed.

"Well, hey ho," one of the men said. He was large in the shoulders and chest, thick neck; he wore jeans, a T-shirt, and a ball cap. "Look who's feeling all nice and clean."

Andy sized up the men. Besides the big guy who was apparently the ringleader, there were two older men, fifties, thin but tightly wound. Both had beards and graying hair pulled back into ponytails. The other two were younger, less than thirty. One couldn't have been more than twenty—he barely had facial hair—and was thin and soft. He appeared nervous but intense; a film of sweat glistened on his face. The other sported a goatee and close-cropped hair. He was wiry and lean, athletic.

Two of the men held shotguns.

Andy clenched his fists and tightened his jaw. He wondered how many he could take out before a shot was fired. But they had the girls, and he didn't want any harm to come to them. He'd have to move carefully, patiently, and wait for the opportune time to present itself. When it did, he'd show no mercy.

The ringleader held Missy by the arm as if she were an insolent child. "Amber told me there was a freak in town, but I never expected this. Hoowee, we got a regular circus clown here, boys."

Amber. The waitress.

Andy stood his ground, moving neither forward in a show of aggression nor backward in an act of submission. "Let them go."

The ringleader laughed. He looked around at the other men. The man holding Belle, one of the older men, pulled her closer to his side and put his arm around her shoulders. "Or what?"

"Let them go," Andy said again. He stared hard at the ringleader, ignoring the older man's question.

The older man repeated, "Or what?"

Andy scanned the men again, meeting their eyes. Something odd about the young guy on the end. He held neither of the hostages nor one of the guns. He stood with his arms hanging loosely at his sides. His eyes seemed hollow, like the lifeless eyes of a shark. Dead to kindness, dead to any kind of conscience. Dead to the world. Andy felt like he knew the man from somewhere.

"Maybe he didn't hear ya, Moe," the ringleader said.

Moe squeezed Missy's arm, bringing a short yelp from her. "It's your move, freak."

"It's your move," Andy said. "I can stand here all day."

The ringleader smirked and looked around at the other guys. "Here that, boys? We got ourselves a regular standoff. Freakshow here thinks he's John Wayne."

"Maybe we should just cut him down," the wiry man with one of the guns said. "Like in those old westerns."

Andy shifted his eyes between him and the other older man with the other shotgun. Both appeared comfortable with their weapons. They were seasoned hunters, military veterans, or both. Of course, The Event had forced many to become comfortable handling a weapon.

Taking a quick survey of the area, Andy noted a thin-trunked maple fifteen feet to his right. The tree stood tall and straight, nearly forty feet high, its skeletal branches reaching out in every direction. The ground around the tree was loosely packed and dry as sand. He also noted the ground was littered with stones, leaves, and twigs. The group of men stood about twenty feet away. The SUV sat with the pickups, blocked from any kind of escape forward or backward.

Andy met Belle's eyes. She knew what he was thinking and nodded in agreement. It was the only chance they had. He'd get only one attempt and he hoped it worked. If it didn't . . .

As if they had practiced the choreography a hundred times, Andy again eyed Belle. She convulsed and shrieked. Her performance was more convincing than Andy imagined it would be and succeeded in drawing the attention of the men away from Andy long enough for him to bend and pick up a golf-ball-sized rock. In one smooth, precise movement, he threw the rock at one of the gun-toting men. It struck him square in the side of the head. The man grunted and slumped to the ground. The gun clattered to the dirt.

Continuing his sideways momentum, Andy spun and dodged behind the tree as the other shotgun discharged. He had only a second or two. He placed both hands on the trunk of the tree, shoulder-height, and pushed with every ounce of strength he had. His feet slipped on the dry ground, but still, he pushed, his muscles so taut he worried they might tear from their anchors. The shotgun discharged again, but the concussion came at the same time the tree's trunk snapped just above the ground, and the tree toppled like a felled giant.

The tree crashed to the ground with a cacophony of snapping limbs and cracking wood. The earth trembled, and a cloud of dust rose into the air twenty feet, obscuring the activity around the tangle of splintered, broken timber.

Andy rushed to the site. When he was still fifteen feet away, Belle and Missy broke from the debris and headed, hand in hand, for the SUV. The blast of gunfire broke the silence. Belle spun and collapsed to the ground. Missy fell beside her, nearly landing on top of her.

Andy stopped, frozen. No. It didn't happen. He tried to move but couldn't. He needed to. A voice screamed in his head for him to move his feet, to go to Belle and Missy and protect them, but time seemed immovable, and with it, the events around him.

Missy ran her hands over Belle's body. She was hollering something. He heard it but couldn't understand what she was saying.

Suddenly, a blow came to the side of Andy's head and knocked him over. The world went black. An instant later, light came rushing back . . . along with an intense throbbing. Two men stood over him. The older man who had held Belle and the younger, athletic man who had one of the shotguns. He had no gun now.

Andy rolled and tried to get up, but they were on him like wolves, kicking and punching, cursing and grunting. He continued to roll to get away from their assault and eventually managed to climb to his knees and launch himself at them.

The violence that unfolded was something Andy was glad he would not remember in detail. He was so full of anger, of hate, of rage, that he allowed—even welcomed—the darkness lurking in some deep cavernous corner of his soul to find freedom and fully express itself.

The men never had a chance. Bones broke, flesh tore, blood flowed. And when Andy had finished and stood panting, the two men were unrecognizable.

Missy wailed. "No!"

Andy spun to find the young man standing in front of Missy, shotgun pointed at her head. Missy knelt beside what appeared to be the lifeless body of Belle, one hand on the girl's head.

"You killed her," Missy screamed. Tears flowed down her reddened cheeks.

The man tensed his muscles. Andy knew what would come next. There wasn't time to rush him and wrestle the gun from him. He was a good twenty feet away. As soon as he heard Andy's advance, he'd pull the trigger. Andy didn't want to witness Missy's death. But before he could turn, fire spewed from Missy's mouth and engulfed the gunman. He stumbled back until his legs buckled. The writhing and screaming that followed only lasted seconds before the man fell silent and motionless.

Chapter 21

She was dead. The girl was gone.

Belle.

The tears could not flow hard enough to dampen the pain Missy felt. She'd been holding Belle when she exhaled her last breath. That final grasp for life as it caressed the girl's lips. She was just a kid; she had a whole life before her.

How could this happen? Why? Who were these men?

Missy allowed the sobs to choke past her raw and burning throat. It had happened again. The fire. She could not control it.

There was so much she could not control.

Her life was no longer her own, it seemed. The trek north, the multiple attempts on her life, the fire—were they all orchestrated by someone or something outside her realm of control? She was a pawn at the mercy of some greater force. *The* greater force. She needed to trust, to have faith she was in hands that cared for her and loved her, but it didn't seem that way. She felt like a target and had good reason to doubt.

Anger washed over her. Not because of what she'd been thrust into, not because she'd become some freak in her own right, vomiting fire and taking lives, but because Belle was too young to die. Like this. Here in the woods. At the hands of such evil men. It wasn't right. It wasn't fair. It wasn't love.

Love would not allow this to happen.

Love would have spared the kid's life, given her a chance to grow up, to live, to find love for herself.

This was cruel.

· · · · · · ·

Andy ran to Missy and Belle. Maybe . . . maybe Belle was not dead at all, only unconscious. Maybe the shot hadn't been fatal, and she could be patched up. They'd need to get her to a hospital.

Missy lay across Belle's motionless body, sobbing. When Andy arrived and dropped to his knees, she said, "It happened again, didn't it?"

Andy stroked Missy's hair. Her cheeks and forehead were smeared with dirt. "Yes."

With numb hands, he felt Belle's neck for a pulse. Nothing. She lay in a puddle of blood. Both eyes were slightly opened; her lips blue and parted. She was gone.

The words landed like boulders in Andy's mind.

Belle. Was. Gone.

Missy sobbed harder. "Why? Why did they do this?"

Andy had no answer. He had no idea why they were being stalked, hunted like fugitives. He had no answers for how their pursuers kept finding them. He put his hand on Missy's shoulder, but she brushed it off. The sobs came in great coughs now and racked her thin frame. She managed to bark out words between sobs. "Why are they trying to kill us?"

After a few seconds, Missy fell into Andy's arms and buried her face in his chest. He held her close and stroked her hair. They sat in the dirt. Andy had nothing to say. No answers for Missy. Anger and sorrow washed over him and collided like waves in the surf. He knew what Missy hadn't yet realized: they weren't trying to kill *them*; they were trying to kill *her*.

The old man's words came back to him again: *The girl . . . this is about her. All of it. She's something special.*

Something special. So special that she must be dangerous to someone, a threat. And that someone has the resources to track them down and keep the vigilantes coming.

They needed to find the nameless old man again . . . or hope that he'd find them. He had answers. He knew what was going on. What was it he said? I'll see you in Boston? Where? When? The man spoke in riddles.

Missy's sobs had calmed some; she placed a hand on Belle's head. "She was just a kid."

"I know."

"She didn't deserve this."

"I know."

"What are we gonna do?" She turned her face upward.

With her swollen eyes and red cheeks, Missy looked as helpless as a lost child. Andy's heart ached for her. She lived in a world of darkness populated only by sounds and smells and explored by the tips of her fingers. He was glad she couldn't see Belle at this moment and glad she hadn't witnessed the violence he'd unleashed on their assailants. She'd unleashed her own brand of violence, and it was probably best she hadn't witnessed that as well.

"We need to bury her and get out of here," Andy said. "We don't know if there are more coming."

Missy's eyes darkened and her face tightened. "More? How? Why? Why can't they leave us alone?" The tears started again.

Andy stood and helped Missy to her feet. "I don't know. But we'll figure this out. I'm going to search the trucks for a shovel."

She turned her face up. "We can't bury her here."

Andy paused to allow Missy to figure out the predicament herself.

She interpreted his silence correctly. "Right. I'll stay here with her."

Andy found a shovel in the back of one of the pickups and dug a shallow grave for Belle about fifty yards into the woods. The ground was dry but loosely packed.

When Belle's body was in the grave and covered with dirt and rocks, Andy told Missy about the old man and the meeting they'd had at the bar. He didn't tell her, though, about what the man had said about her. She had enough to worry about and didn't need to carry the burden that his statement brought with it.

He put his arm around her shoulder and pulled her close. "C'mon. We need to get to Boston. We'll get answers there."

Chapter 22

After The Event, sanctuary cities were set up throughout the country. Twenty in all. Most of the country was devastated, the population decimated. The National Guard, in its attempt to bring under control an animal population that had gone rogue, had destroyed major portions of the nation's cities and suburban areas. When everything—without explanation—returned to a new sense of normal, the rebuilding began. The twenty sanctuary cities were the first to receive federal funding to clean up, repair, and rebuild. In the northeast, Boston, New York City, and Philadelphia were the designated sanctuary cities. People flocked to those cities by the thousands—some homeless looking to start a new life, many suffering from both physical and emotional trauma, most having lost someone they loved either to The Taking or to the animals. The national mourning continued for years.

When Andy and Missy arrived at the edge of Boston, they were stopped at a checkpoint. All the sanctuary cities had checkpoints. With so many refugees filtering in from around the country, these cities needed to maintain order and to monitor who came and left.

The checkpoint along Route 1A was nothing more than two state trooper cruisers and three troopers. One of them stopped the SUV with a raised hand and walked around to the driver's side.

"Afternoon, folks." He scanned the interior of the SUV with steady, serious eyes. "Driver's license and registration, please."

Andy handed the trooper his license as Missy rifled through the glove box for the registration. When she found it, she handed it to Andy who passed it along to the trooper.

"Kentucky, huh?" the trooper said, studying Andy's license.

"Yes sir."

"Why are you coming to Boston?"

"To meet a friend."

The trooper lifted his eyes and stared at Andy, taking in the full image of Andy's deformities. "Friend, huh?" He glanced at the registration. "Your name isn't on this registration."

"I know. We borrowed it from a friend. Reliable vehicles are hard to come by in some areas."

"A friend in Pennsylvania?"

Andy nodded.

"What's this friend's name?"

Andy froze. He had no idea. He hadn't looked at the registration before handing it to the trooper.

Missy leaned closer to the open window. "Actually, they're friends of mine. Rick and Diane Summers. They live near Harrisburg."

The trooper handed the license and registration back to Andy. "All right, folks. Enjoy Boston. And stay out of trouble, you hear?"

"Certainly, officer," Andy said.

He rolled up the window and moved slowly through the checkpoint. On the other side, he turned to Missy. "How did you know that?"

She smiled, the first one she'd given Andy since they left the campground. "While you were showering, Belle rooted through the glove box and told me the car belonged to Richard Summers of Mechanicsburg. She said that was near Harrisburg."

Andy reached across the seat and touched Missy's hand.

"Belle is still helping us," Missy said.

....

They made their way down Washington Street, past residential homes and small businesses, past parks and strip malls, saying very little to each other. The old man had said he'd meet them here in Boston, but where? Boston covered nearly ninety square miles. How could they possibly find him?

Near the center of town, Andy noticed signs for Boston Common, a community park. He followed West Street to Tremont, then circled the park until he found a parking place on Beacon Street near Frog Pond.

"Why did we stop?" Missy said.

"I think we both need some fresh air," Andy said. "We need to collect our thoughts."

"Agreed. Where are we?"

"Boston Common."

"The park?"

"You've been here?"

"No. But I've heard of it."

To walk through Boston Common one would think The Event never happened. The grass was as green as leprechaun blood, and the trees were fully leafed and full of life. The city must have spent considerable money to irrigate the entire park. An oasis in the middle of a desolate and barren world.

Near the pond, Missy stopped and pressed herself against Andy's side. She drew in a deep breath. "What does it look like? It smells fresh and green."

"It looks green. Everything is green. Do you have memories of what the world used to look like before?"

"Those are the only memories I have."

"How do you imagine it, then?"

"Green. Lush. Fertile. Full of life. For the past ten years, I've smelled and felt nothing but death and dryness and . . . nothingness. This is different. It's alive."

"Yes, it is. Very much so."

Andy led Missy around the pond to a bench. Shortly after The Event, the news networks had transmitted images of bodies floating in this pond. There'd been so much slaughter in Boston, in most of the large cities. Before the animals went nuts, humans had created the chaos. Rioting. Looting. Murders. Mostly driven by fear of the unknown and unexplained. Then the animals arrived. Dogs, cats, coyotes, wolves, even bears. They migrated to the most populated areas where the prey was most concentrated.

"What does the pond look like?" Missy asked.

"It's shallow, just a couple feet. Maybe two hundred feet by fifty feet. The water is clear, like a pool. Can you hear the kids splashing in it?"

"I can hear them laughing. It's nice to hear laughter, isn't it?"

It *was* nice to hear laughter. Andy's life had never been one conducive to laughter. His life—what he could remember of it— had been marked with hardship and adversity. "It is."

"You know, I don't think I've ever heard you laugh," she said.

"I don't laugh much. I don't think I've ever laughed much."

A voice from behind them startled Andy. "You used to laugh a lot."

Andy turned and saw the old man standing by himself, hands in his pockets.

Missy turned her face toward Andy. "He's here?"

"Yes."

The man came around and stood before them. "You laughed a lot as a child. You were happy then." He motioned toward the bench. "Mind if I sit?"

"Not at all," Andy said. "Are you Ben Baxter?"

The old man sat and crossed his legs. He shook his head thoughtfully. "No. Ben was taken with the rest of them. I knew him, though. Knew him well. And your mother. And you when you were a boy, no higher than my waist."

"How did you know them?"

The man ran his gaze over the pond and pursed his lips. "That's another story. For another time. I knew Ben from our seminary days. He introduced me to your mother." He grew quiet for a moment, let his eyes shift to the trees, then to the sky. "Did I mention he was taken?"

"You did."

"I guess I did."

"What's your name?"

"Clem."

"How'd you find us?" Andy asked.

The old man looked at Andy. "We'll get to that. I don't have a lot of time. They'll be here soon."

Chapter 23

"Let's start with this," Andy said. "Who exactly are you?"

"A friend. I got to know your mother through Ben. I'm sorry she's gone."

"She spoke of Ben many times but never mentioned anyone named Clem."

"She would have known me as Clement. But I don't suppose she would have mentioned me. No real reason to."

"So what does that have to do with us?" Missy asked.

Clem paused and surveyed the area again. He took his time, pausing to watch a couple of walkers about a hundred yards away. Finally, he turned his attention to Andy and Missy again. "You're probably wondering about your . . . abilities."

Andy reached for Missy's hand but kept his eyes on Clem. "My mom told me I was different."

Clem nodded. "That's one way to put it. You are very different." He stroked his chin and furrowed his brow as if contemplating how to proceed. "Are you familiar with any of the popular Bible stories? Creation, the flood?"

"Sure. My mom took me to Sunday school."

Clem looked at Missy. "Are you, young lady?"

"Yes. I am."

"Good. Are you familiar with the Nephilim in Genesis?"

Andy had never heard the word before. "No."

"The sons of God," Missy said.

Clem nodded. "Yes. The sons of God. Fallen angels."

"Their offspring were giants, men of renown."

"They were Nephilites," Clem said. "The product of unholy unions between women and the sons of God."

"Fallen angels," Missy said.

"Demons," Andy added.

"The Nephilim were special. They were"—Clem glanced at Andy—"different. Men of great strength who did remarkable things and became known for their might and superhuman abilities. Many think they are the source of ancient mythological heroes and even the superheroes we have today."

Andy's skin burned and tightened along the back of his scalp and neck. His pulse quickened and throbbed in his throat and ears. His mother had rarely spoken of his father. But when she had, it was usually to note how evil he was.

Clem stared at Andy. "When your mother was in college, she met a man who claimed to love her. He didn't. He was evil and had evil intentions. You were conceived, which was something your mother was never sorry about. But your father. He . . ."

"He was a demon."

Clem sighed. "Yes."

"Which makes me a Nephilite."

Missy squeezed his hand. "Different."

At that moment, Andy could have sworn the earth froze and time stood still. Nothing else registered. Not Clem's voice. Not Missy's touch. Not the laughter and squeals of the children playing in the pond. Not the dogs barking in the park. Nothing but that word echoing through his mind: *different.*

He looked at Clem. "I'm part demon."

"You're human," Clem said. "It's the only way you could have been conceived. Somehow, some way, demons found a way to take on human form. To appear human in every way. And then it happened again. And you weren't the only one conceived."

"There are others like me?"

"Yes."

"Trevor?"

"No. There's more going on here than you can imagine."

"I can imagine an awful lot," Missy said.

Clem tightened his lips, then said, "Not this." He looked around again, allowing his gaze to linger on a few folks walking in the park. One man in particular, a young guy walking a Doberman on the other side of the pond, seemed to catch his interest. He glanced at his watch. "We don't have much time." He spoke quickly and deliberately. "The book of Revelation talks about—"

From across the pond, the man with the Doberman shouted something, then broke into a run, the dog keeping pace with him.

Clem frowned, scratched the back of his neck. He looked from Andy to Missy to the running man, then back at Andy. His face tightened and deep furrows creased his brow. "You two need to get out of here."

Andy didn't move.

"Now," Clem said. The intensity in his eyes said he was serious. "Go." He pointed behind them, toward their SUV. "Get to Portland. Look for Amos. Or he'll find you."

"Portland?" Andy was confused.

Missy stood and tugged on Andy's arm. "Maine."

Clem glanced at the man now rounding the far corner of the pond. "This may be the last time we'll speak. Revelation eleven. Now go." He turned and ran toward the man and the dog.

Andy took Missy's hand and led her away from the bench and toward the SUV. At Beacon Street, he turned in time to see Clem and the man clash at the edge of the pond. The dog launched itself at Clem, taking hold of his leg. Walkers and waders screamed and scattered.

"What is it?" Missy asked, concern etched on her face.

"We need to go." Andy looked around and spotted three men heading their way. They seemed disinterested in the commotion occurring at the pond and singularly focused on Andy and Missy. All three were large, shaved heads, sunglasses. Bouncer-types. They wore khakis and polo shirts. Combat boots. When their gaze met Andy's, all three broke into a run.

"Come on." Andy had only a second to decide whether to stay and fight or run and find a place to regroup. He chose to run. He gripped Missy's hand tighter and pulled her along.

Across Beacon Street they ran, then east toward the Old State House. The men followed, quickly closing the distance between them.

Chapter 24

Outside the Old State House, a crowd of protestors had gathered. Shoulder to shoulder, they packed the sidewalk. Some held signs that read No More Sanctuary Cities; some shouted chants about every town needing money.

With Missy's hand firmly in his, Andy pushed through the crowd. The pursuers followed but were slowed by the pressing protestors. Andy used the mass to put space between them and the threesome of bouncers.

"Stay close," he said to Missy as he shoved past a man spouting obscenities.

Once they broke free from the crowd, Andy pulled Missy along as he ran down Beacon Street. At the corner of Beacon and Bowdoin, he glanced behind him and saw the bouncers emerge from the mob.

"Keep moving," he said.

"Are they still behind us?"

"We haven't lost them yet."

Andy knew there was little chance of losing the trio in Boston. They were too close. He needed to be careful not to get cornered, not to allow the bouncers to trap them. He needed to find a secluded place to confront the men.

Ahead, at the corner of Beacon and Tremont, Andy and Missy went left. There, a parking garage. It may provide the isolation they needed.

"C'mon," Andy said. "Parking garage."

"Why?"

"We need a place away from the public." He knew she'd understand why.

A concrete ramp led to a subterranean garage. Dimly lit, it provided good cover. Andy knew the threesome had seen him duck into the garage. He pulled Missy along to the first row of cars and crouched behind a large black Chevy SUV.

"Stay here," he said to her. "Stay quiet. I don't want you involved, you hear?"

She nodded.

"No matter what, don't stand. I'll come back for you."

Her eyes wide and darting about, lips parted, she nodded. Andy started to pull away from her, but she grasped his wrist. "You're my angel. My guardian."

. . . .

When Andy left her, she held her breath as she listened for his footsteps. She whispered a prayer for him. Andy was no demon; she was sure of that. He wrestled an inner demon, but didn't everyone? He was different, for sure, but not in any way that he thought.

Andy's footsteps grew fainter, then silent. He was hiding somewhere, waiting to ambush their pursuers. She hated the thought of a confrontation. Her imagination could be very vivid, and in her mind, she saw all sorts of exaggerated images. She hoped and prayed the ordeal would be short.

Again, she prayed for Andy's safety.

. . . .

Andy waited behind a concrete barrier, listening for the men's footsteps to approach and draw near. The men were there. He could hear them stepping lightly, but they said nothing to each other. He couldn't tell how tightly they were grouped and wouldn't know until he sprang on them. Obviously, the closer they were, the better it would be for him—especially if they carried weapons, which he assumed they did.

As their footfalls padded closer, Andy drew in a deep breath and tensed his muscles. He'd have to make quick decisions once he revealed himself. He had the element of surprise, but that advantage would only last a second or two. In that time, he had to choose which man to attack first and how to transition to the others. There would be no time to think. His moves had to be instinctual, reflexive. He'd have to strike hard and fast and finish the job before they could coordinate their movements.

They were now within ten feet of his hiding place. He breathed again and imagined the fight in his mind—each move, each countermove.

When they were within five feet, he sprang from behind the barrier with all the ferocity and speed of a cougar surprising its prey.

The lead man swung his head around, eyes as round as golf balls. He'd been pointing his handgun away from Andy's location.

Andy had the advantage he'd hoped for.

....

Missy heard the initial confrontation, a grunt, then a fleshy thud. Someone, not Andy, hollered, cursed. More grunts and thuds, shoes scuffing on concrete. Metal clattered. Then a breaking sound, like a dry stick snapping when you stand on it. A man hollered and cursed again.

The skirmish seemed to last a long time, but the sound of it was carried out in bursts of activity, smacking flesh, grunts and moans, curses. Then . . . a gunshot echoed off the concrete floor, walls, ceiling.

Silence.

Someone spoke, but she couldn't make out what was said.

Andy groaned. Another burst of activity ended with a solid, wet thump. The floor beneath her shuddered.

Silence again that stretched on for seconds.

Then "Missy." Andy's voice was weak and thready. "Missy."

She crawled from behind the vehicle. "Andy?"

"I need help."

"Keep talking." She got to her feet, staying crouched, and followed the sound of his voice.

"I've been shot."

She found Andy lying on the concrete. His abdomen was wet and sticky. The smell of sweat and blood was strong. Panic crept into her chest and tightened. Andy had been shot. What if he died? What would she do? She ran her hands across his chest. So much blood.

"I need to get out of here," he said.

He was right. He couldn't stay there. Someone would come along, find him and the others, and call the police.

"Okay. Can you walk?"

"I—I think so. You need to help me up."

She tugged on him as he pulled on her. After a lot of grunting and groaning, she got Andy to his feet. He put his arm around her shoulder as she led him to a pedestrian area of the garage. There he collapsed and moaned.

"You need a hospital," Missy said.

"I'll be okay."

"No, you won't." She touched his abdomen again. "You're losing a lot of blood."

"I just need to rest."

"You need a doctor."

Missy heard footsteps, dress shoes on concrete. She hushed Andy.

The footsteps drew nearer, stopped, paused, then scurried off.

"What was that?" she asked.

"We gotta get out of here."

"What was that sound? Was someone there?"

"A man saw us. He saw the bodies. He got a good look at me. Ran off. He'll get the police."

Her voice trembled again. "What do we do?"

"We need to find a car."

Chapter 25

The burning was intense, like someone had crawled inside his body and lit a fire. His left side spasmed and cramped. The bullet must have hit a rib. Every breath sent shards of glass through his muscles.

Missy leaned over him and stroked his hair. Her face was pale and wet with sweat. A few strands of hair stuck to her forehead. When she spoke, her voice quavered. "I need you to get up. Can you do that? You're too big for me to carry or drag."

She was right. If they were to escape, he'd have to get up again. Walk. Stumble. They needed to find a car and exit the garage. Get to Portland.

He needed a hospital. The gunshot. The open wound. The blood. But he couldn't go to a hospital. The police would be looking for him. They'd find him, arrest him. And what would happen to Missy?

He remembered how quickly the burns on his face had healed, unnaturally so, but they were superficial wounds. This was different. The bullet had torn flesh and possibly organs, most likely broken a bone or two.

"Hurry," Missy said. There was panic in her voice, urgency.

He had to move, to will himself to contract his muscles, endure the pain, and stand. Walk. And then . . . drive.

Sweat soaked his forehead and ran into his eyes. Andy grunted and grasped Missy's hand so she could help him stand. Pain shot through his flank like a spear. The edges of the wound were raw and nerves were exposed.

Once standing, he took a second to clear the fog from his mind and let his vision clear. The pain had nearly knocked him out. And then it was one agonizing step in front of the other. They'd have to search the cars, look for one that was unlocked. Belle had shown him how to start a car without a key. It took some dexterity but wasn't too difficult.

When they reached the first car, Andy leaned on the hood and scanned the parking area. A car that had some years on it would be best. Inconspicuous. And Belle had told him that newer cars with all their electronics and computers were more difficult to start.

There, he spotted a '90s model Ford Taurus. Gray. "Missy, four cars down. Check the doors."

In the distance, the faint wail of sirens cut through the normal city noise.

"Hurry," Andy said.

Missy felt her way along the cars and checked the door of the Taurus. "Locked."

"What about the back doors? The other side?"

She followed the contours of the car with her hands and checked all the doors. "Nope."

Andy ran his eyes around the garage. "C'mon, c'mon."

"Okay. Straight across from that one, other side of the aisle. I'll lead you. Try it."

It was a black Chevy Malibu. Early '90s. In pretty good shape. Missy scurried across the aisle and felt for the vehicle.

"One more to your right. Yes, that one."

Missy felt for the door, tried the handle. It opened easily. "Got it."

Andy forced himself to move, to walk. Each step sent jolts of pain through his body until he became nauseated and thought he'd vomit.

The sirens grew louder.

At the car, he slid in behind the wheel and felt beneath the steering wheel. The wires were right where Belle said they'd be. In a matter of seconds, he had the engine purring and shifted into reverse. In the mirror, he saw the reflection of the police cruiser's flashing lights on the concrete supports.

Andy worked the gearshift and stepped on the gas. The engine revved and the car lunged ahead. By the time they'd rounded the first corner in the garage and started up the exit ramp, the cruisers arrived.

Andy didn't stop or even slow at the garage's exit. The car's nose thudded against the concrete as it came off the ramp and entered the street. They almost collided with another driver who promptly blew the horn and gave an appropriate gesture.

Andy didn't know his way around Boston. He hadn't the slightest idea which way he should turn when they came out of the garage. But he knew they needed to get out of the city.

Flashing lights in the mirror caught his attention. The police. They'd targeted him and followed him out of the garage. He needed to make quick work of this before the cops coordinated and boxed them in. There would be no escape then.

Pushing farther down on the gas, Andy blew through a light that had just turned red and made the next left. He needed to stay on secondary streets where he'd be more concealed. The cops would barricade the primary arteries and interstates, but he hoped they'd overlook or not have the manpower to cover every secondary and tertiary street in the city.

He took the next right onto Bowdoin Street, then left onto Derne, then left onto Hancock. If he could get back to Beacon Street, he could head west. Not the direction he wanted to go, but he had to get off the peninsula. He was sure all those routes would be blocked or at least monitored.

Andy checked his mirrors. He didn't see any flashing lights. Maybe he'd lost them already.

Maybe not. Two cruisers turned onto Beacon. Two blocks behind him.

Soon the police would get a chopper in the air, and then the net would tighten.

Chapter 26

Andy made a sharp right onto Massachusetts Avenue. A block later, it added a lane and crossed the Charles River. He pressed on the gas, the engine whined, and the car accelerated. Weaving in and out of slower traffic, he crossed the bridge. The cruisers were still behind him, but he'd managed to increase his lead. He saw no flashers ahead where the bridge met the north bank of the river. At the intersection, he did not slow for the yellow at Memorial Drive. Instead, he accelerated, and the car's speed increased to nearly fifty miles an hour.

The red light would slow the cruisers, allowing him to put even more distance between them and him. He then made a right onto Vassar and buzzed through the campus of Massachusetts Institute of Technology. He turned left onto Main Street, then right onto Windsor. The cruisers were no longer behind him. He'd managed to lose them for now.

At the next intersection, he made a left onto Hampshire Street and then a right onto Columbia. They were in the heart of Cambridge. Town houses lined the street, pedestrians milled about. Some talked with neighbors; some wandered aimlessly. The trees that once dotted the sidewalks had all been cut down, their stumps reminders of the way life used to be.

"Did we lose them?" Missy asked.

Andy checked his mirrors again. "I don't see anything, but that doesn't mean we lost them."

"They won't give up that easily."

"Nope. One wrong turn and we could run right into them."

She turned her head in his direction. "Then make the right turns."

"We need Belle."

"In more ways than we know."

He drove a couple blocks, then made another right. Carefully checking his mirrors at every turn, they made their way north through Prospect Hill to Spring Hill and eventually to the campus of Tufts University.

"We need to find a new car or take to foot," Andy said.

"Are you in any shape to walk distances?"

Stabbing pain had shot through his abdomen with every turn of the steering wheel, but the bleeding had stopped, and the pain had dulled over the course of the last couple miles. Could he be healing already?

Along College Avenue, Missy said, "If you see someone walking, slow down and pull over. I want to ask them something."

"There's a woman up ahead." A college-aged woman with shoulder-length blonde hair pulled back in a ponytail walked with a small dog. Andy slowed the car beside her, and Missy rolled down her window.

"Excuse me."

The woman stopped and looked their way, surprised by the interruption. She looked both ways, then cautiously approached the car but did not enter the road. "Yes?"

"My friend and I are hoping to do some hiking. Is there anywhere around here for that?"

The woman paused for a moment. "About a mile or so north of here is the Middlesex Fells Reservation. I've never been there, but lots of the students go there on the weekends."

"Great. You say about a mile north?"

"Yeah, just over the Mystic River."

The Mystic River. They'd have checkpoints all along it. Every road heading north would be monitored.

"Okay. Thanks so much," Missy said.

She rolled up her window, and Andy pulled away from the woman.

"The river," he said.

"I know."

"We need a new car."

"Will it make a difference? You're bleeding."

His shirt was soaked with blood from the abdomen down.

"How are you feeling?"

"A little better. The pain isn't as intense."

He steered the car into a parking lot near a baseball diamond and found a parking space to the far right. When the car was stopped and the engine off, he lifted his shirt. Crusted blood covered his abdomen. The entry wound was black and scabbed with dry blood.

"How's it look?" Missy asked.

"Not bad. I mean, it looks like a gunshot wound, but all things considered . . . I think it's healing already."

She reached out her hand. He took it and gently placed her fingertips on the wound. She pulled her hand away. "Does it hurt when I touch it?"

"Not really. It's tender, but the sharp pain is all but gone."

She sat quietly for a few seconds, processing. "You're different," she finally said.

"I think that's the understatement of the day." He looked around the parking lot. It was only about half full, mostly with newer model cars and SUVs. A few students exited the gym in sweats, toting duffel bags. More entered. Too much activity here, too many eyes. "I need a change of clothes," he said. They'd have to walk past the checkpoint. Maybe they could slip across the river at a narrow spot and cross the barricade unnoticed. It was their only option.

A group of four male students approached a cluster of cars not fifty feet from where they were parked. Andy cracked his window so he could hear what they said.

An Asian guy with a duffel bag slung over his shoulder broke away from the others and walked to a late model Nissan Sentra. "Let me just ditch this here, and we can head on over." He opened the car door, tossed his bag into the back seat, then joined the other three. As he walked away, the car chirped twice signifying he'd locked the doors.

Andy grunted.

"What is it?"

"Clothes," he said. The guy was about his size too. "But the car just locked."

"Can't you break the lock?"

He could, yes. But it would set off the alarm and draw all kinds of unwanted attention. He could pry the door open enough to slip the antenna in and pop the lock, avoiding the alarm, but the very act itself—a man with a bloodied shirt wedging open a car door—would appear suspicious and would no doubt draw the attention of any passerby.

There had to be another way.

He checked the back seat of the Malibu, hoping the owner had left a change of clothes. Nothing. "Stay here," he said. He checked the area and waited for a woman to walk by on the nearby sidewalk. When the area was clear, he slipped out of the car and went around to the trunk. Popped it. Inside was a suitcase. He unzipped it and found a stack of neatly folded pants and polo shirts. He checked the size on the shirts. XXL. Too big for him. But it would have to do. Quickly, he slipped off his T-shirt and pulled one of the polos over his head. Again, he checked the area. A threesome of women exited the gym and walked toward the parking lot. Andy grabbed a pair of pants and got back into the car.

"What did you find?" Missy asked.

"Jackpot. Shirts, pants, everything I need."

His pants had blood on them, so a change was necessary. With much effort, he slipped off his pants and pulled on the new pair. Three inches to spare at the waist. He needed a belt.

"Okay," he said to Missy. "Ready. We exit the car very normally and head around to the back, okay? I need a belt out of the trunk. These pants are way too big."

"Got it." She nodded and opened the door.

Andy retrieved a belt from the suitcase and slipped it on. He took Missy by the hand and led her away from the car. "We need to head north. Toward the river."

In the distance, sirens howled and drew closer. Andy tensed.

Chapter 27

"Quickly," Andy said. He grasped Missy's wrist and led her along College Avenue to the first right, Franklin. That led them to Main Street. They were off campus now. The sirens grew closer.

Andy didn't know what kind of description of him the police had. He wasn't sure if it included the condition of his face. The guy in the parking garage had seen Missy, though, so the police were looking for a man and woman. He also would have told the police that the man appeared to be injured. He had no way, of course, of knowing Missy was blind. In addition, the police wouldn't know that they were traveling on foot. This was all to their advantage.

On Main Street, they headed north, Andy trying to look as casual as possible, holding Missy's hand loosely. The pain in his abdomen was dull now and only stabbed when he twisted or contracted his abdominals.

"Just keep walking," he said to Missy. "We're doing fine."

The sirens increased in number. They must have located the car in the gym's parking lot. In the distance, he heard the faint thrumming of a helicopter.

"Let's walk a little faster," he said.

They hurried past large residential homes and empty storefronts. Past apartment buildings and parks. A block away, a police cruiser turned onto Main Street and headed toward them.

Andy pulled Missy into the side yard of a large home. "Kneel down and act like you're working in the garden," he said.

A few seconds later, the cruiser rolled by. Andy didn't lift his head.

When the area was clear, they hurried down Main Street until they reached South Street, which ran parallel to the Mystic River.

"We need to find somewhere to wait for dark," Andy said. It was the only way they'd make it across the river unseen. The police had checkpoints along the bridges crossing the river.

"What time is it?" Missy asked.

"A little after noon." The sun would set in seven hours.

Where South Street met Winthrop and Winthrop crossed the river, there was a small grove of trees with thick undergrowth. Because of the nearby source of water, the trees were fully leafed, and the grass grew green and soft. The river ran narrow—not more than fifty feet—at this point and shallow enough to walk across.

Breathless, Andy led Missy to the grove and sat her by a tree. "We'll wait here. You okay with that?"

She put her hand on his. "We'll be okay."

"I'm glad you're so confident."

• • • • • • •

To pass the time, Andy and Missy talked about the events that had led them to hide among the brush and trees along the banks of the Mystic River in Medford, Massachusetts. A police cruiser had rolled by soon after they found their spot, then another about an hour later, but other than that, the traffic that passed was of the ordinary sort: cars, delivery trucks, SUVs, pickups. None of the drivers had slowed to take note of the two fugitives in the grove. Andy and Missy had concealed themselves well.

As the sun set, the temperature dipped a few degrees, and Missy shuddered. Andy scooted closer to her and put his arm around her shoulders. "Do you mind?"

She shook her head. "No. It's okay. The air is chilly."

"You never finished your story about Ron," Andy said.

Missy sat quietly for a few long seconds.

"You don't have to if you don't want to," Andy finally said. He could only imagine the pain she lived with every day. Losing her sight at the hands of that man. Losing her mother during The Event. Then having to deal with Ron again.

Missy sighed. "No. I guess I probably need to. I've never talked to anyone about it." She nestled closer to Andy as if finding some protection from the memory in the warmth of his body. "Years went by after The Event, and I heard nothing from Ron or about him. I thought he'd either moved on to another location or died. I think I'd convinced myself that he must have died, that he must have ticked off the wrong person and finally got what was coming to him."

"But he wasn't dead."

"No. One night I found some shelter in an office building. Some of the offices were empty, so I broke in and found a warm corner. It was such a cold night. I remember that. There was thunder in the distance, too, the real rumbly kind." She paused and laced her fingers over her knees. "I woke up and there he was, standing over me. I could sense him. I could smell him. He smelled the same as he always did, even after all those years. Like he'd never left. He hit me hard, then tried to rape me. I put up a fight, but he was so much bigger than me and stronger. I was no match for him."

Andy closed his eyes and pulled her closer. "I'm sorry."

Missy shook her head. "He didn't rape me, though. He would have. I have no doubt about that, but . . ."

"But what?"

"The thunder. It was loud. Close. So close it seemed to shake the building. I thought at the time he'd been struck by lightning. I could smell the burning flesh. I left him there. I was so afraid

I was somehow responsible and would be found and tried for murder. I didn't think anyone would believe that he'd been struck by lightning while trying to rape me. What were the chances." She stopped and sighed.

"But it wasn't lightning."

"Nope. I had the same taste in my mouth, the same burning. At the time, I thought it was some kind of residual effect from being so close to someone who'd been struck. Believe me, I replayed it over and over in my mind trying to make sense of it, to explain what had happened and how I'd felt afterward. That was the first time it happened."

"The fire."

"The fire." She turned her face toward him. "I killed him."

"It was self-protection. He would have killed you."

"I killed Colin's friend and Trevor and that other guy too. I'm a murderer."

Andy squeezed her. "No. You're not. You acted in self-defense. Each of those guys would have killed you if you hadn't done that." He was right but doubted she'd see it that way. She was too sensitive. Her heart hadn't become callous like Andy's; it was soft, sincere. If there had been a way to defend herself and spare lives, she would have done it.

Missy rested her head on Andy's chest, and they sat in silence until the sun dipped low in the sky.

Just after sunset, when darkness had crept into the area like a thief, Missy said she had to use a bathroom.

Andy stepped out from his cover and scanned the area. Most of the traffic had ceased after six o'clock, and what little there was would be apathetic to two people strolling down the street after dark. They'd have to find a gas station or fast-food joint. Some place where they could enter and leave without notice.

"C'mon," Andy said, extending his hand and taking Missy by the wrist. "We'll find something."

Two blocks west, they came across a gas station, Rodney's Gas N Grub. The bathrooms had an exterior entrance around the side of the building. The sign by the door instructed prospective users to inquire about the key at the register.

"Stay here," Andy said. "I'll get the key."

He entered the gas station and approached the counter. The guy behind the desk was young, thin, and had a Middle-Eastern look to him. He did not look like a Rodney. He eyed Andy suspiciously.

"Can I get the key to the bathroom?" Andy said.

The guy looked around. No one else was in the store. "Keys are for customers only."

"I just gotta use the bathroom, man."

The cashier took a step back from the register. "Customers only," he said again.

Andy turned and headed to the refrigerators at the back of the store. He should get some food and drink for Missy and himself anyway. He grabbed four bottles of water, a bag of pretzels, some granola bars, and two bananas at the counter.

....

When Andy left, Missy stood with her back pressed against the building. The brick was cool and rough beneath her hands. She hoped the area was dark enough that she would not be visible to any vehicle driving past. The last thing she needed was a cop dropping by to ask a few questions.

She tapped her foot on the concrete. What was taking Andy so long? Her bladder begged to be emptied. Her stomach growled. They hadn't eaten anything all day.

A car rolled by and Missy froze, held her breath. Her heart thumped in her throat. The car moved slowly but did not stop.

Missy exhaled and slapped the brick with an open hand. They had to hurry. C'mon Andy. She inched farther toward the back of the building, away from the road.

Again, she wondered who was hunting them. And why? And how had they so efficiently coordinated their movements that Andy and Missy couldn't travel to the next town without being confronted or chased or attacked?

Another force seemed to be at work, an unearthly malevolent power with influence and control. But what power? And again, why was it targeting her?

She had no answers, of course. Neither did Andy. Clem might have had some, but he was gone now. All they knew was that both she and Andy were different, some sort of mutants with unexplainable powers.

Another vehicle rolled by. The heavy sound of its tires indicated it was a truck. As before, she froze and turned her face away from the road.

Andy better hurry up.

·······

"Will that be all, sir?" the cashier asked.

"And the key to the bathroom," Andy said.

The cashier reached under the counter and retrieved the key. "For customers only," he said with a smile. "Please return it when you're done."

"Thanks."

Andy took the items and key to where Missy waited.

"What took you so long?" she asked.

"The bathroom is for customers only. I had to buy some stuff."

"Food?"

"Yeah. And water."

"Great. I'm famished."

He placed the key in her hand. "You have to use the men's room."

"Really? Aren't they, like, gross and stuff."

"Probably. I didn't want him to know I had someone with me. The cops are looking for a man and woman, and they may have talked to the store owners around here." He opened the bathroom door. "I'll make sure it's clean for you."

She smiled. "Such a gentleman."

When Missy emerged from the bathroom, Andy handed her the bag of food and said, "Wait here."

He entered the gas station to return the key. The cashier again eyed him up and down.

Andy placed the key on the counter. "Thanks, man."

"Thank you for your patronage," the man said. "Are you from around here?"

He was suspicious. No doubt the police had indeed paid him a visit and given him a heads-up. "Just passing through," Andy said. "Thanks."

He left the store, rounded the corner of the building, and took Missy's wrist. "We gotta move. I think he's onto us. He may contact the cops."

"Where are we going?"

"Across the river."

Chapter 28

They crossed at the narrowest, shallowest point they could find, upriver about a quarter mile from the gas station. Heavily leafed trees cloaked both sides of the river in deep night shadows, and the water was only about a foot deep. The water was cool but not cold, and it moved slowly, gently splashing at their legs.

On the other side, they sat on the bank, hidden by trees and wild shrubs, and dried their feet.

"We should only be about a half mile from the reserve," Andy said.

"As the crow flies."

"Right. A little longer following roads."

"We need to find some place to sleep," Missy said.

Andy knew they couldn't hike all night. The air would get chilly. They needed to find a warm, dry place to bed down and get some sleep. They had a long trek ahead of them.

"We will," he said. "Then tomorrow we'll find another vehicle and head for Portland."

"Clem said to find Amos there."

"Yes. Amos." Whoever he was. And Andy had no idea how they'd find one man in a city the size of Portland.

Missy pulled her shoes on and tied the laces. When she finished, she paused and turned her face toward Andy. "What happened to Clem?"

An image of the Doberman lunging at Clem flashed through Andy's mind. He didn't need to give Missy the grisly details, but she deserved to know the truth. "He gave his life for ours."

She sat quietly for a few minutes, her eyes bouncing around his face as if in her mind she could see him perfectly, without the scars, without the doubt, without the fear. Studying him. Taking in the nakedness of his soul. Finally, she said, "Will we make it?"

"To Portland?"

"No, to wherever we're ultimately headed."

"I don't know where that is."

"But will we make it?"

He thought about that. "Clem said you're special, that all of this is about you, so, yeah, I suppose we will."

"What's so special about me?"

"He didn't get a chance to say."

"Revelation eleven."

"You know it?"

"Nope. I've always been fond of the Old Testament. The stories are great."

"I'm not too familiar with any parts of the Bible."

"We need to find one."

They did. Answers to some of their most pressing questions would be found in the eleventh chapter of Revelation. But Missy's statement held a much larger challenge than the simple words implied. There were no Bibles left. Very few, at least. A year or so after The Event, Christianity was declared a "religion of hate" and outlawed in the United States and much of the world. Practitioners were criminalized. Existing Bibles were collected and destroyed; the printing of new Bibles was prohibited. Some survived, of course, but finding one fully intact was nearly impossible. "We will," Andy said, though he doubted his words as soon as they passed his lips.

She sat quietly again, hugging her knees to her chest. The sound of the river meandering by was relaxing. Fatigue tugged at Andy's eyelids. They could sleep there, but the temperatures would drop, and being so near the water was not safe. Besides, when morning came, they'd be exposed. They needed the cover of the reservation. They'd have to emerge sooner or later and find a vehicle, but for now, they needed to lie low until the cops gave up their search.

"How do you feel about what Clem told you?" Missy asked.

"About me being part demon?"

"He didn't say that. He said you were all human."

"My dad was a demon, so what does that make me?"

She put her hand on his arm. "Human."

He wanted to believe her, wanted to believe what Clem had said about his father becoming human, but he couldn't. The dreams he had, the things he saw—he knew now that they weren't random thoughts and images thrown together by his subconscious filing system. They were memories, imprinted on his DNA. The creatures he saw were real. They were not of this world, not even of this physical realm.

"If I'm human, how can you explain this?" He lifted his shirt and placed her hand on his abdomen where the bullet had pierced his flesh. It was now fully healed and sealed with scar tissue. A remnant of pain remained, but it too was mostly gone.

She said nothing.

"And how do you explain my strength, my stamina, my ability to get the snot beat out of me, then get up and keep walking like nothing happened?"

She pulled her hand away and said in a soft voice, "I don't know."

Andy stood. "I really don't want to talk about this anymore tonight. We need to get moving. I'd like to some place to bed down before the night gets too old."

He helped Missy to her feet, and they set out north, toward the Middlesex Fells Reservation.

Twenty minutes later, they'd reached the reservation. They walked along Border Road for another half mile, noting a few parking areas where morning hikers would leave their cars. At one of the areas, Andy led Missy down a hiking trail until they found an outcropping of rocks.

"This will have to do," he said. "We'll have our backs against the rocks and bury ourselves in leaves. You okay with that?"

Missy nodded. "I've slept in worse places."

It pained Andy to think of Missy on her own for so long, wandering around in darkness, feeling her way through the world and navigating its dangers without protection. But somehow she'd managed.

Andy made a nest of sorts from dried leaves and held Missy close so they could share each other's warmth. "How did you make it on your own?"

She didn't answer right away, and he thought she'd fallen asleep. But finally she said, "The righteous walk by faith."

He didn't fully understand what she meant, but he was tired and didn't feel like probing the statement. Instead, he pulled her closer and closed his eyes. Images of Dean Shannon wanted to penetrate his mind, but he fought them off. As they retreated, images of his mother's blackened form pushed past them, but he resisted them as well. They'd haunted him long enough. He focused on Missy, on her face, the softness of her skin, the smell of her hair. The feel of her body nestled against his. And he realized that what he felt for her was more than some platonic sense of being her protector. He cared for her. Deeply. He loved her. She'd worked her way into his hardened and soiled heart; she'd brought some light into his heavy, dirty soul. She'd given him hope, a reason to fight the demon within. He'd been tottering on the precipice of hopelessness when she'd found him in that drainage pipe, and meeting her had made all the difference.

Her deep sleep-breathing relaxed his muscles, and he gently stroked her hair. He could spend every day with her. With his back against the rock and the weight of Missy's body against his chest, Andy drew in a deep breath. He didn't know what the future held; he had no idea what they'd find in Portland, but he knew he could face it with Missy by his side.

Eventually, he allowed himself to drift to sleep.

．．．．．．．

The man stood in the woods, concealed by darkness and night shadows, and watched the duo sleep. They'd had such a hard journey, but he felt no remorse and no sympathy for them. They should both be dead by now. And if he'd had his way, they would be dead.

The girl was frightened and confused. Her world of darkness had become so much more dangerous, so much more mysterious, so much more uncertain. Her faith wavered. He could feel it, sense it, hear it in her voice and questions.

The freak was frightened and angry. He was afraid of his shadow, what he was, what he could become—would become—if he surrendered and allowed his true nature to assume control.

And this was how the man would break Andy. In his dreams. He'd torment him with visions of what he truly was, of what resided inside him. He'd show him the ugliness of his soul, the darkness of his heart. He'd tempt him with power, lust, and the world of pleasure that lay just beyond his reach. Within his reach, if he so desired.

And then he'd take the girl from him and break him one final time. That would be the catalyst that drove him to surrender, to yield control and authority. He'd become a pawn then, a very useful idiot.

．．．．．．．

At some point during the night, Andy awoke with a chill. Missy slept soundly, her breathing deep and even. She'd been so tired

176 / Mike Dellosso

but hadn't complained once. He supposed it took much more effort for her to navigate this world.

She was remarkable.

He pulled her close and adjusted his arm so it draped over her shoulders and down her arm. She stirred and mumbled something unintelligible. The feel of her body aroused some deep desire in him. In the dead of that quiet night, thoughts he did not want to entertain assaulted him. She was there for the taking. How easy it would be in the woods at night. She may even enjoy it. Maybe she shared his feelings. Maybe she'd entertained thoughts of being with him, holding him, kissing him. She had no idea what he looked like.

Andy almost woke her but instead pushed those thoughts from his head. They didn't stay away long. Missy stirred again; her aroma enticed him. He became very aware of every curve of her body, of the placement of his hands and her hands, of the gentleness and gracefulness of her form.

He could take her. He wanted to take her.

Again, though, Andy forced the thoughts from his mind. They were not his thoughts. He cared for Missy and would never hurt her, would never take advantage of her. He needed to get some sleep. They'd have a long day of travel when the sun rose.

He closed his eyes and pushed out the uninvited thoughts that wanted to shove their way in. Eventually, he grew tired of the fight against sleep and willingly succumbed.

·······

He was afloat in a dark sea, lying prostrate on a raft of thin wood. The raft drifted up and down, to and fro, following the crests and troughs of the throbbing water. Beneath the raft, something moved, something writhed. Andy gripped the edges of his tiny vessel. Above, the sky was ridged and loomed close. Gray clouds churned and swirled, promising a thunderous storm.

Suddenly, a hand broke from the water—a woman's hand, gray and thin, the angle of each joint protruding into leathery flesh. It groped about until it found Andy's leg, just below the knee. Then another appeared, and another, all the same, all groping about. Andy tried to escape their probing but it was useless; there must have been a dozen of them. One grabbed his wrist, another his thigh, and another his bicep. Each pulled at him, tugging him toward the inky water.

A flash of lightning ripped through the sky, followed by a roaring clap of thunder. The movement of the sea intensified, the crests reaching ten feet now. The tiny raft rolled along, but the height and valley of each wave threatened to spill Andy from the fragile vessel.

And the hands, there were more now, pulling at him, tearing his flesh. Their nails dug into his skin and drew blood. And the more blood that flowed, the more hands appeared as if they were drawn there like sharks to the aroma of the wounded.

Andy struggled to free himself, struggled to remain on the raft. But he was losing his grip. His arms ached; his hands cramped. His fingers could no longer feel the rough surface of the wood.

Eventually, the fight would be lost, and he would slip into the dark waters forever. Whatever gruesome beings were attached to those hands would have their way with him, and he supposed he would become one of them, looking for the next victim to float along.

He told himself he would not let go, regardless of the pain, regardless of the fatigue. He would hold tight and remain on the raft. But he knew it was a promise he could not keep, not without help. He would lose the will to fight and eventually give in, surrender, succumb to the relentless pull.

·······

Another man stood in the forest, yards from the sleeping Andy and Missy. They were out of view but not out of mind. Andy battled unseen forces and creatures from another dimension. His soul was the prize, and the enemy fought viciously for it.

The man stood behind a tree and prayed. Soon he would intervene, but for now, his support would have to remain unheard by human ears and unseen by human eyes.

． ． ． ． ． ． ．

A foot had nudged her awake, heavy, like a boot. Missy stirred and wrestled to gain a bearing on where she was and who had awakened her. Andy? No, he slept next to her.

"Hey." A man's voice. Deep. Firm.

Missy rubbed her eyes, pushed away from Andy. Fear gripped her throat, and her dry mouth couldn't produce saliva to swallow. She elbowed Andy, but he didn't even stir in his sleep.

"Miss?" The man again.

Missy stretched out a hand in front of her and waved it back and forth. "Stay away."

Leaves crunched as the stranger shifted his stance. "Ma'am."

She elbowed Andy again, shook him. "Andy."

． ． ． ． ． ． ．

A voice wafted over the water then, a woman's voice. Missy. It was barely audible over the roar of the sea and booms of thunder, but he knew it was Missy. She called his name.

"Andy."

He had to hold on for her. She needed him, and he needed her too.

"Andy."

They were meant for each other. Neither fate nor coincidence had pushed them together, had led her to him in that drainage pipe.

"Andy."

There was something more there, something providential about their meeting.

"Andy!"

Andy startled and awoke. A leaf scratched his face and he pushed it away. It was light outside. Morning. Missy nudged him. "Andy."

Andy cleared his eyes and looked up. A man towered above them. He wore a uniform.

Chapter 29

"What're you two doing?"

"Excuse me?" Andy said. He was still trying to clear the sleep fog from his head and rid himself of the images in his dream.

"There's no overnighting in the park." The man was tall, thin, clean-shaven. He wore a green uniform with some sort of outdoor insignia on it. A park ranger.

Andy sat upright. "Oh, sorry." He held his head in his hands. "We, uh, we—"

A voice from Andy's left interrupted. "Oh, there you are. Thank God we found you." An elderly man approached. Small, thin, dirty gray goatee. His clothes were baggy but not ill fitting. His eyes were the clearest blue Andy had ever seen. "Boy, I thought we'd lost you two." He turned to the park ranger who now looked very confused. "Officer, this is my niece and her boyfriend. We were hiking last night, and they got caught out here after sunset. Must've gotten lost."

The ranger turned to Andy, then glanced at Missy.

"She's blind, sir, you see," the old man said. "Needs a guide at all times."

"She—she wandered away from me," Andy said. He had no idea who this man was but gathered he was there to help. He'd play along for now. "I had to look for her. By the time I found her, it was dark. We got turned around. I didn't want to stumble around in these woods all night, so we decided to wait for help. We must've fallen asleep."

The ranger turned to Missy. "Miss? You want to add anything?"

Missy faced the ranger; her eyes danced around his face but never focused on it. "I'm sorry, sir."

The ranger put his hands on his hips and scanned the woods. "You know your way out?"

"Sure do," the old man said. "Got my truck back in the parking lot."

The ranger looked Missy and Andy up and down. "You two look like you could use a hot shower and change of clothes. Go on. Be more careful next time, you understand? For your own safety."

Andy stood and helped Missy to her feet. "Thank you, sir."

The old man shook the ranger's hand. "Thank you for finding them. I was so worried. We all were." Then he turned to Andy. "Let's go."

They walked in silence until they reached the truck and got in, shut the doors.

Andy turned to the old man sitting behind the steering wheel. "You mind telling me who you are?"

He turned the key, bringing the engine to life, and shifted into drive. "Someone who just saved your hide."

"Why?"

"Why what?"

The road cut through the leafless forest in wide turns and bends. There were few straightaways as it followed the curve of the terrain.

"Why did you save our hides?"

"And how did you know where to find us?" Missy said.

For a handful of long seconds, the driver focused on the road that lay ahead. "What happened to Clement?"

Missy turned her face to Andy and felt for his hand.

"You know Clem?" Andy asked.

The old man tightened his jaw. "What happened to him?"

Missy faced the driver again. "You changed the subject."

"I did." He paused and turned onto another road that took them deeper into the reservation. "I'll answer all your questions as best I can, but first I need to know what happened to Clement."

"He died," Andy said. "As best we can tell. Yesterday in Boston. He—he gave his life for us."

Missy squeezed Andy's hand.

The old driver fell silent and serious again. His jaw muscles flexed rhythmically as if he were chewing. Finally, he said, "Did he give you the message?"

"What message?"

"Did he tell you who you are?"

Andy didn't want to answer. He didn't know this stranger and didn't know if he could be trusted.

Missy apparently knew something Andy didn't. "He told Andy who he was," she said. "He started to tell us about me, but we got . . ."

"Interrupted," Andy said. "He told us to read Revelation eleven."

"Did you?"

"We don't have a Bible. No one does."

"How do you know about all this?" Missy asked.

The man paused, glanced at Missy, then Andy, then back to the road. Outside, the sky was brightening, and bars of shadows and light now striped the road. "I'm a friend."

"That doesn't tell us much," Missy said.

"Did Clement tell you where to go?"

Andy said, "Portland. He told us to find some guy named Amos."

The old man nodded slowly. "Amos. Yes, that makes sense."

"So who are you?"

"Tony. I'm here to take you to Portland."

Tony turned right onto a road partially barricaded with a Road Closed sign. He glanced at Andy. "It's closed for construction. Still passable at this time of day."

"How did you know about Portland?" Missy asked.

"You two think you're alone but you're not. There's a whole network of folks in place to make sure you get where you need to be." He slowed the truck and turned right onto a road that climbed straight up a steep hill. "Thing is, there's a whole network of *other* folks at work to make sure you don't get there."

"Why?" Missy asked. "What's so special about us?"

Tony lifted his eyebrows. "You haven't noticed yet?"

"That's why we're being hunted? Because we're different?"

"Not because you're different, but why you're different."

"I'm not following."

He pointed to the glove box. "Open it. There's a Bible. Revelation eleven."

Andy opened the glove box and retrieved a small worn copy of the New Testament and Psalms. But before he could open the book, a terrible crunching sound shook his eardrums, and the truck lurched forward to the right.

Chapter 30

The truck veered off the road and skidded into an embankment with such force that Andy's seat belt broke, and he slammed into the dashboard. The world momentarily went black, and an alarming ringing settled in his ears. When he came to, he noticed three things.

Missy was slumped in the seat. Her belt had held, but she'd apparently hit her head on the dash with enough force to knock her unconscious.

The windshield had shattered and littered the interior with tiny pieces of glass. Tony lay on the ground in front of the truck, face bloodied and his right arm twisted behind him at a very uncomfortable angle.

Smoke poured from the engine compartment, but through it, Andy could make out the form of a semi sitting on the roadside, its brake lights glowing red.

Andy rubbed his eyes and head. A thick haze clouded his mind, jumbled and muddled his thoughts. Where had the semi come from? Who drove it?

There's a whole network of other folks at work to make sure you don't get there.

He looked over at Missy. A single trickle of blood ran from a cut on her forehead, over the bridge of her nose, and down her cheek.

Righting himself, Andy scanned the area. Nothing but forest on either side of the truck. The sky was clear, the sun still low. From around the back of the semi, a figure appeared, a man. He carried something in his hand.

186 / Mike Dellosso

A gun.

There's a whole network of other folks at work to make sure you don't get there. Portland.

If Andy had hoped the accident was just that, an accident, his hopes were dashed at the sight of the man with a gun. He had to move; he had to get Missy out of the truck.

He unbuckled her seat belt and pulled her into his arms, then opened the door. By the time he tumbled out and onto the ground, the man had reached the front of the truck and stood over Tony.

Tony groaned and moved. From his vantage point on the ground, Andy could see only the man's legs. He stood over Tony for a couple seconds, then discharged his weapon. Tony's body flinched, then fell motionless. The gun discharged again.

Andy tried climbing to his feet, but the man was there before he could even get to his knees. He wouldn't toy around with Andy and Missy. He was there to kill them, not take them captive, not torment them. His mission was singular.

The man was young and tall, thin but muscular. His angular face housed two large round eyes. Dark. Lifeless. A shark's eyes. He grinned but said nothing. A man of few words and all action.

There was no time to plan, no time to talk or plead or bargain. Instinct had to govern his movements. Without taking time to calculate or weigh the risks, he pushed off the ground with both arms and swept his foot toward the gunman's legs. His foot connected with the man's ankle with enough force to knock the man off balance.

The gun discharged.

Missy shrieked.

The man went down and hit the ground.

Andy had to move quickly. He followed the direction of his momentum and continued his spin while he stood. From his position on the ground, the man raised the gun again, but Andy was there. His leg swung around and caught the man's hand, dislodging the gun and sending it skidding across the ground. Without hesitation, Andy was on the man. Behind him, Missy choked and gurgled. He stole a quick glance. She groped at her neck, both hands red with blood.

She'd been hit. She needed help. She needed Andy.

The gunman lunged at Andy and struck him along the left side of the face, but the blow had little effect. Andy dropped his weight on his attacker's body and head-butted him squarely in the nose. The man tried to roll away, tried to fight back, but Andy's attack was relentless. He rammed his forehead into the man's face over and over again.

But the man would not give up. He continued to fight and struggle. Eventually, he put enough space between himself and Andy that he could drive his knee up and into Andy's groin. Andy toppled off, nausea spreading into his abdomen. The man climbed to his feet but not before Andy could get upright. Both men faced each other. The gunman's swollen nose dripped blood. His eyes were wild and hate-filled.

On the ground, Missy continued to struggle for breath. She was choking on her own blood. Andy had to finish this, or Missy would never make it.

Seeing that Andy was distracted by Missy, the man threw himself at Andy and caught him in the chin with a solid fist. The blow was so hard it pushed Andy back and spun him nearly in a full circle. The gunman had incredible strength. Like Trevor.

But Andy remained on his feet, and as the man lunged again, Andy sidestepped and caught him with an elbow to the face that stopped his advance. The man stumbled back. Andy followed with a blow to the jaw, an elbow to the nose. He grabbed the man's head and butted the bridge of his nose again.

In such proximity, though, the man could get both hands around Andy's throat. Andy delivered a series of blows to the man's trunk, but it had no effect. He had only one option. He grabbed the man's head and thrust both thumbs into his eye sockets. The man screamed and squeezed his eyes closed but did not loosen his grip. His hands pressed on Andy's trachea, threatening to crush it. Andy tightened his neck muscles and pushed his thumbs deeper until he could feel the curve of the eyeballs.

Missy stopped moving.

Andy let out a primal scream and jammed his thumbs even deeper into the man's eye sockets. The man's grip loosened, and Andy shoved him away, following that with a powerful upward blow to the nose.

The man staggered back, wavered on rubbery legs. His head teetered loosely on a swivel. Finally, his legs gave way, and he crumpled to the ground.

Andy rushed for Missy. She no longer choked or gurgled. She'd given up the fight. Her hands lay limply by her sides. The right side of her neck was torn open, the artery severed. Blood no longer flowed.

Missy was dead.

Chapter 31

Andy cradled Missy's limp and lifeless body in his arms and allowed the tears to flow. Questions, like smoke, swirled through his head. How could he allow this to happen? How could God allow this to happen? She was supposed to be special. She had a purpose. All of this had been about her. And now . . . and now she was gone. Her neck ripped open and the life drained from her.

He sat like that for nearly half an hour, holding her, crying, questioning. He'd failed her. He alone was supposed to protect her. Get her to Maine, to Portland. That was his only job and he couldn't do it.

Finally, Andy allowed Missy's body to slump to the ground. He got up, went back to the truck, rummaged through the cab, and looked for the Bible. Maybe it held the answers to his questions. There, under the seat. He flipped through the pages until he came to the book of Revelation. Chapter eleven.

Andy placed a shaky finger on the page and read . . .

Then I was given a reed like a measuring rod. And the angel stood, saying, "Rise and measure the temple of God, the altar, and those who worship there. But leave out the court which is outside the temple, and do not measure it, for it has been given to the Gentiles. And they will tread the holy city underfoot for forty-two months. And I will give power to my two witnesses, and they will prophesy one thousand two hundred and sixty days, clothed in sackcloth."

Three years. But what did that have to do with Missy?

These are the two olive trees and the two lampstands standing before the God of the earth. And if anyone wants to harm them, fire proceeds from their mouth and devours their enemies. And if anyone wants to harm them, he must be killed in this manner.

Andy swallowed past the tightness that had constricted his throat. Heat spread up the back of his neck and settled into the base of his skull. Fire proceeds from their mouth. Devours their enemies.

Fire.

His hand shook harder, so hard, in fact, that he had to stop reading for a moment to steady it.

These have power to shut heaven, so that no rain falls in the days of their prophecy; and they have power over waters to turn them to blood, and to strike the earth with all plagues, as often as they desire. When they finish their testimony, the beast that ascends out of the bottomless pit will make war against them, overcome them, and kill them. And their dead bodies will lie in the street of the great city which spiritually is called Sodom and Egypt, where also our Lord was crucified.

But how could this be Missy? How could she be one of these witnesses? She was dead now. The prophecy was void. It couldn't be her.

Then those from the peoples, tribes, tongues, and nations will see their dead bodies three-and-a-half days, and not allow their dead bodies to be put into graves. And those who dwell on the earth will rejoice over them, make merry, and send gifts to one another, because these two prophets tormented those who dwell on the earth. Now after the three-and-a-half days the breath of life from God entered them, and they stood on their feet, and great fear fell on those who saw them.

Andy's heart thumped in his throat now. Dead three days and rise again. But she was dead now. This prophecy had not yet happened. Again the questions were there, swirling, swirling, swirling. Andy suddenly felt dizzy and had to sit on the ground.

And they heard a loud voice from heaven saying to them, "Come up here." And they ascended to heaven in a cloud, and their enemies saw them. In the same hour there was a great earthquake, and a tenth of the city fell. In the earthquake seven thousand people were killed, and the rest were afraid and gave glory to the God of heaven. The second woe is past. Behold, the third woe is coming quickly.

Andy closed the book and held it in his hands as if it were made of the most fragile Chinese porcelain. He looked Missy's body over. There was no life in her. He'd checked her pulse several times to make sure he hadn't missed anything. The bullet had hit the carotid artery in her neck, and she'd bled out. Simple as that. Clem must have been wrong. Tony too. Missy was not the one.

But what about the fire? People didn't breathe fire. There was no natural or scientific explanation for it. She wasn't some freak of nature, some genetic mutation gone weird. She could breathe fire and devour her enemies, just like the Bible said.

But she was dead now. No getting around that. Maybe she was one of the witnesses it spoke of. Maybe it was Andy's job to protect her, and since he'd failed, the prophecy was now obsolete, or someone else would fill her position.

Andy crawled over to where Missy's body lay and put his hand on her head. Her flesh felt cool. For the first time since his mother died, he bowed his head and prayed.

If the Almighty had been expecting something terribly insightful and moving, he would have been disappointed. Andy's prayer was simple and quick, but it was a prayer nonetheless. And it was a start.

When he finished, he felt no different. The earth did not move under his feet; the clouds above did not part. No sunshine warmed his skin. His flesh did not break out in goose bumps, and he experienced no palpitations of his heart. If he had been expecting any of that, he too would have been disappointed. Instead, he sat on the ground and stared at nothing in particular. How long he sat there he did not know. But when the sun began its downward arc, he decided it would be best to get out of the woods and continue his trek north. Maybe Amos would know what to do. Maybe he would have answers.

Andy stood, bent at the waist, and scooped Missy's body into his arms. He couldn't take the pickup. It was too banged up. The driver-side front tire was bent at an odd angle, and the engine still puffed a steady stream of smoke. He'd have to take the rig.

Inside the cab of the truck, he carefully placed Missy's body on the back seat, stretched out the legs, and placed the arms across her waist. He stepped back and shook his head. She appeared to be sleeping—except for the gaping wound in her neck and the dried blood covering half the body.

Andy got behind the wheel, donned his Stetson, and started the engine. It grumbled and growled and finally came to life. The rig vibrated from the rumble of its six massive cylinders. He put it into gear and steered onto the road. During his time on the ranch, he'd learned how to drive a rig and even got his commercial driver's license.

The truck had a nearly full tank of fuel and was equipped with GPS navigation that guided Andy back to I-95 headed north. Portland. Amos.

Andy drove a little over two hours before reaching I-295, which would take him into Portland. In the back seat, Missy's body lay still. Faux sleeping.

Andy turned off the highway and onto Route 1. There, he stopped at a small local diner, Alice's Treats & Eats, and forced food into his belly. He was not hungry. He was not tired. He felt nothing. He chewed the burger he'd ordered, drank the soda in the glass. He thought of nothing. He stared at the couple across the aisle until the older man stared back at him with an unfriendly scowl.

When he'd finished the food and used the restroom, Andy returned to the truck, climbed in, and sat behind the wheel.

He needed to keep moving. Needed to get to Portland. Needed to find Amos. If Amos even existed. Maybe Missy's death had thrown the whole thing off. Maybe there was no Amos now. Maybe his very existence depended on Missy's survival and arrival in Portland. And now that she was gone, the whole thing was a bust.

What would he do if it was a bust? If he had no purpose? What purpose did he have now that Missy was gone? And what was he going to do with her body? He couldn't just dump it somewhere. He couldn't bury it. Or could he? Maybe he could find a funeral home in Portland or a hospital and leave it by the door. But that didn't seem fitting either. He hoped to find Amos and recruit his help.

Andy turned around in his seat to make sure the body was okay, that it hadn't, unbeknownst to him, rolled off the seat and onto the floor.

But the body wasn't there. Missy was gone.

Chapter 32

Missy found herself seated in a patch of dry, brittle grass. She wasn't sure how she got there. She'd been shot. In the neck. She remembered the pain, the blood, the struggle to breathe.

The feeling of suffocating.

And then . . . she was in the field. She felt like she should be tired or hurting or scared, but she was none of those things. In fact, she felt great. Physically, she couldn't remember a time when she felt better. She felt her neck. There was no injury, no entry wound, no torn muscles or blood vessels. Just smooth, soft flesh. Mentally, her thinking was clear and sharp. She understood what her purpose was; she saw the path she needed to follow. Spiritually, peace enveloped her like a warm blanket. She was secure and confident. She was not alone and never would be.

Missy held her face toward the sky. She would not be afraid. She had something to do, and Andy would be part of it. He didn't know it yet but he would very soon.

·······

Heart banging against his sternum, Andy slid out of the truck and looked around the parking lot. Thoughts raced through his head like a roller-coaster at full speed. Did someone take the body? And if so, why? Where would they take it? Had the police caught up with him? Were they waiting for him? Watching him even now to see what his next move would be? Maybe she wasn't dead in the first place? No. She was. He was sure of it. She had no heartbeat, her flesh had turned as blue as her eyes, and when he'd lifted her into the truck, rigor mortis had already stiffened her head and neck.

There were a few cars in the parking lot, a motorcycle, and a full-size pickup with oversized tires. Behind the diner lay an open, dry grassy field and beyond that, a wooded area. A gas station and auto body shop sat across the street. A couple of men perched on stools and talked outside the station. One drank soda out of the bottle.

Andy crossed the street and approached the men. The sun had yet to dip behind the horizon, so he thought maybe they had seen something.

The two saw Andy coming and stopped their conversation. One of the men had a full beard and the other a mustache. Both appeared to be seventy or older. They looked Andy up and down and awkwardly tried to avoid his face.

"Excuse me," Andy said.

Neither man spoke. Instead, they both stared at Andy as if they'd never seen a man with half his face melted off. At least not this close.

"Did either of you see a woman come out of the truck over there? Or anyone go into the truck?"

They both shifted their eyes to the truck, then back to Andy.

The man with the beard nodded his head slowly. "She with you?"

Andy could see it in their eyes. The doubt. The accusations. Freaked-up guy with a young lady in the back of his truck. Now wondering what happened to her. If human trafficking was bad before The Event, it had become exponentially worse afterward. With local, state, and federal law enforcement's numbers drastically reduced and the government as a whole in disarray, little attention had been invested in matters such as trafficking and prostitution. One would like to think that citizens would band together to put aside such immorality and lawlessness. But too often, these kinds of national tragedies only brought the rotting apples to the surface of the barrel and emboldened them to increase their depraved activity. The Event seemed to have served as a booster shot for immorality.

"Yes," Andy said. "She's a friend."

"A friend," the mustached man said.

Andy glanced back at the truck and scanned the surrounding area again. "Look, fellas, I know what this looks like—"

"And what's that?" the bearded man interjected.

Andy paused long enough to look each man in the eyes. "She's a friend, nothing more. There's nothing weird going on here."

The bearded man waved a hand in the air. "Nothing weird like you got a little thing goin' on with the girl? You holdin' her as your plaything or something like that? Nothin' weird about that. Nope."

Andy tensed his jaw.

The bearded man stood and went chest to chest with Andy. He was every bit as tall as Andy and probably had him by at least twenty pounds. "Look, mister, I don't like to presume things about folks, but you're makin' it very temptin'. When I see a young lady come stumbling out of a truck covered in blood, I get to wonderin'. Wouldn't you?"

Young woman covered in blood. Stumbling out of the truck.

She was alive? Missy was alive? And walking?

Andy's mind went blank, and numbness spread all the way down to his fingertips.

The man must have noticed Andy's confusion and shock. He leaned to the side to keep eye contact. "Wouldn't you?"

Andy snapped back to the present conversation. "Uh, yeah. Yes."

The man turned and looked at his friend, then faced Andy again. "Did you think you killed her? Beat her to a pulp?"

Andy shook his head but barely noticed his own movements. How could she be alive?

"Hey." The bearded man poked Andy in the chest. "Did you do that to her?"

"Uh . . . no. No way. I thought you didn't like presuming things about people."

"Not presumin', son, just askin'."

"She's, uh, she's injured. Badly."

"And you stopped for a casual meal with an injured woman in the back of your truck?"

Again, Andy saw how this looked. But he didn't care anymore. He needed to end this conversation and find Missy. "Which way did she go?" He quickly checked up and down the road but saw no sign of her. She couldn't have gone far.

The man stared at him and said nothing.

"Did you call the police?"

Still, he said nothing. The mustached man crossed his arms and drilled Andy with a narrow-eyed glare.

Andy motioned as if he was going to put his hand on the man, but the mustached guy unfolded his arms and stood, took a step toward Andy. Andy backed off. The last thing he needed was to get into a brawl with these two guys and draw more attention than he already had. Instead, he turned and walked away. He had to find Missy, get her cleaned up, and get out of there.

When he'd crossed the street, Andy glanced back at the two men. Both were still standing, arms crossed, watching him. He went back to the truck to inspect the interior. Maybe some clue there would lead him to where Missy might have gone.

The interior was undisturbed, nothing out of place. No obvious footprints or handprints to even show which door Missy had exited. The blood covering her neck and chest had dried, and there weren't even any dried flakes on the truck's flooring.

Andy climbed down from the truck and looked around. Across the street, the men were still there, arms crossed. They hadn't moved. They wanted him to know they were still keeping four watchful eyes on him.

The parking lot was empty, and no one could be seen for several blocks in either direction. Andy then headed to the back of the building. Rounding the dumpster that sat at the corner of the diner, he stopped; his breath caught in his throat.

Missy was there, on her knees, hands clasped in her lap, face turned skyward, eyes open wide. Andy took a step toward her, and dry grass crunched beneath his foot.

Missy turned her face toward him.

"Missy."

She did not seem surprised at all that he had found her.

"I'm back," she said. "And it's about to begin."

Chapter 33

Andy approached her cautiously. He'd never talked to someone who'd died and come back to life. His skin felt all prickled and tingling. She faced him, her eyes shifting back and forth, mouth slightly open. Something was different about her, something . . . more. He sensed an energy emanating from her. This was not the same Missy he'd allowed to be shot and killed. She was Missy, of course, but . . . more.

Andy knelt next to her and gently touched her face. "Missy, what happened?"

"I was shot. You were there."

"Yes. Yes, I know, and I'm—"

She grabbed his hand. "No. You don't have to apologize. It was part of the plan."

"What plan?"

"*The* plan. It's all different now. I see so clearly."

"Can you see now?"

She smiled. "Not with the eyes of man. With the eyes of faith."

"But you . . . you were dead."

The smile grew bigger. "And now I'm not."

"How is this possible?"

"How is any of this possible? I know who I am."

"The witness."

"Yes. His witness."

Andy helped her to her feet. "We have to get to Portland, find Amos."

"We need to act quickly," she said. "The enemy is here and his army is growing. They're all around us. They'll try to stop us."

"They've been trying to stop us all along."

She stopped and took Andy's face in her hands. "But this will be different. It's about to begin and we must be ready."

"What's about to begin?" He didn't understand this new Missy.

"The end. We need to find Amos."

The end of what? Andy needed more information, more answers to questions he hadn't even asked yet.

But before he could ask, Missy turned her face toward the back of the building. When she spoke, urgency vibrated through her voice. "We need to go. Now."

Andy took her by the hand and led her around the building. They ran across the parking lot to the rig. He opened the door and helped her in. Across the street at the gas station, the two men were gone. Either they'd grown bored of the drama, or they'd left to get help. Andy started the truck and shifted into gear, but before he turned onto Route 1, he heard the growl of engines in the distance. Coming from the south, less than a quarter mile away, a pack of motorcycles barreled down the road. They did not appear to be a friendly gang enjoying a leisurely tour of the northeastern coastline.

"Hold on." Andy hit the gas and the rig lunged forward.

Chapter 34

Andy pushed through the gears on the rig as fast as he could, but the motorcycles were much quicker than the oversized truck trying to accelerate its thirty thousand pounds. In less than a minute, the bikes surrounded the rig. The riders were all men, big in the arms and shoulders. They wore leather vests and chaps over jeans. Stereotypic bikers. Long hair, handlebar mustaches. Lots of ink.

Andy pressed the gas pedal closer to the floor, and the engine roared. He yanked on the air horn, a warning to the burly bikers. But his warnings were either misunderstood or ignored. As long as he kept moving, they couldn't do anything but tag along. But the rig was running low on fuel, and the Portland city limit was quickly approaching. He'd have to slow and obey the speed limit.

The I-295 bridge lay low over the water of the Fore River before the city limits. The truck rolled down the road at seventy-five miles per hour with its motorcycle escort on all sides. Andy thought about running a few off the bridge or maybe hitting the brakes and clearing a few bikers that way. But he decided against it because of the other traffic on the road.

In the passenger seat, Missy appeared relaxed about the current situation.

"You okay?" Andy asked.

She turned her face toward him. "Of course."

She had to hear the rumble of the motorcycles all around them; she had to feel the pressure in the cab of the rig. She had to smell the odor of Andy's stress sweat emanating from his pores.

And yet she was as calm as if they were taking a lazy ride through the Maine countryside.

"Up ahead," she said. "Get off the highway and go right, toward the harbor."

Forest Avenue was the next exit.

"But that'll take us into the city. Lights, intersections, traffic."

"And Amos."

They came upon the exit quickly and Andy took it. He had to slow and eventually stop at the end of the ramp. His two-wheeled escorts stopped as well; the engines of the bikes idled loudly. None of the riders looked at him. Not one even turned his head in Andy's direction. They all stared straight ahead as if nothing could distract them from their mission. They did not appear aggressive in any way either. But there was something strange about them, about their behavior, that sent spider legs down Andy's spine.

When the light turned green, Missy said, "Go right."

Forest Avenue headed straight for a few blocks, then dead-ended at Congress.

"Go right," Missy said again.

"How do you know?"

She smiled. "GPS."

Andy turned the truck right and headed down Congress to Park Street.

"Left," Missy said.

The motorcycles stayed close. There were fifteen in all, and they positioned themselves in front and back of the rig. The drivers showed no antagonism in either their driving behavior or body language. They actually appeared calm.

Park sliced through downtown Portland until it dead-ended at Commercial Street, which ran parallel with the harbor and its assortment of piers.

They stopped at the intersection of Park and Commercial. The bikes idled noisily in front and back.

"Which way?" Andy said.

Missy held up a hand. She turned her head side to side as if she could see the surrounding area—the streets, homes, piers, and warehouses.

Behind the bikes, a pickup honked its horn.

"Got anything?" Andy asked.

"Right," Missy said.

"You sure?"

The pickup honked again. Andy checked his mirrors. The bikers appeared unfazed by the impatient driver.

"Yup."

He shifted the truck into gear. The bikers in front seemed to know the plan all along was to go right. They led the way.

A couple blocks down Commercial, Missy said, "Here. The warehouse."

The bikers slowed and turned into the parking lot of what appeared to be an abandoned warehouse on a land pier that jutted into the Fore River. Andy followed.

The warehouse was made of brick. Some of the bricks were cracked and broken. Long narrow windows, at least a story high, lined one side of the building. Some of the panes had been broken out and never replaced. Beyond the warehouse and pier, a swollen, orange sun touched the horizon.

Andy stopped the truck and let the engine idle. He was unsure of this plan even if Missy was totally on board with it. The motorcyclists stopped their bikes in a sloppy circle around the truck and shut off their engines. One by one, they dismounted and entered the building.

· · · · · · ·

They had arrived. Finally. After all that had transpired the past few days, they were finally here, in his grip. He would take them here, manipulate them, kill them. But he would do it in style.

He would not kill the girl. As much as he wanted to, he needed to practice restraint. He would allow Andrew to kill her. And he would make him want to kill her. By the time he was done with the freak, he'd eat out of the man's hand like a dog.

He would take his time, though. Make it last until midnight. The end of one day, the beginning of another. It would be symbolic of the end of one era and the beginning of another. This was his time. He called the shots. He ruled and all obeyed him. He only needed to get the two mutants out of his way. And he needed to do it with an exclamation point.

The man's skin crawled and tingled with anticipation. He could barely contain his elation. Not in two thousand years had he felt this kind of nervous excitement.

·······

"What do we do?" Andy asked Missy.

Her expression had changed. The smile that had parted her lips for most of the trip through Portland had vanished. Her jaw was slack, her brow tense. She held her hands in tight fists on her lap.

Andy touched her arm. "What's wrong?"

"We have to go inside," she said. Her voice was tight and cracked mid-sentence.

"You sure? I mean, we don't have to."

She nodded. "Yes, we do. It's part of the plan." She grabbed his hand and held it tight, turned her face to him. "Andy."

"What?"

"No matter what happens in there, you have to believe in who you are, who you were made to be."

"What do you mean? What's going to happen?" This new Missy spoke in riddles. He didn't have the knowledge she assumed he had.

"No matter what is said or done, you have to be strong.

Believe." Her face grew tense; her eyes stopped bouncing around and narrowed. "You must believe. Be who you were meant to be. You must trust the truth, not your feelings."

"Who was I meant to be, Missy? I don't understand."

She loosened her grip and her face relaxed. She stared straight ahead again. "You were meant to be great. And good. We have to go inside. It won't begin until we do."

"What won't begin?"

She tightened her fists again. "I told you. The end." This time her voice held an edge that revealed her irritation with his obtuseness.

Andy killed the truck's engine, and they both sat in silence. After a few seconds, he said, "Are you ready?"

"You need to be ready," she said. "Remember what I said. There won't be anything easy about this."

Andy opened the driver's side door and slid out of the seat. He went around to the passenger side and helped Missy down. They held hands as they crossed the crumbling parking lot and entered the building.

Inside, there were no lamps, but the light that filtered through the grimy windows cast a dirty glow on the cavernous interior. The bikers lined the far wall as if they were awaiting instructions.

At once, the locks engaged on the door Missy and Andy had just come through and on the large overhead doors on the far side of the warehouse. The sound of metal engaging metal echoed through the empty building.

Missy stepped closer to Andy and grasped his hand tighter.

Chapter 35

On the north side of the building, a door opened, and a man stepped out of what appeared to be an office space. He was tall, lean, muscular. Middle-aged. Dark hair and narrow, deep eyes, long face. Full lips. He wore a pair of wrinkle-free gray slacks and a light-blue dress shirt. Business casual.

The man walked to within thirty feet of Andy and Missy and stopped, clasped his hands behind his back.

He stared at them without saying a word for a full thirty seconds before Andy said, "Who are you?"

The man's mouth curled into a devilish smile. "You want to know who I am. How ordinary."

An odd comment from an odd man. Andy didn't feel right about this guy, and he could tell by the way Missy held his hand that she felt the same way.

"Who I am," the man said, "is insignificant, don't you think?"

Andy said nothing.

"Who you are," he said, then shifted his dark eyes to Missy, "now that's of great importance."

The man knew who Missy was, or at least he thought he knew. Andy glanced over the man's shoulder at the bikers still lining the wall. They hadn't moved. If they chose at some point to attack, he'd have a tough time fighting all fifteen of them.

"You need not worry about that," the man said.

Had he read Andy's thoughts? Looked inside his mind and found the fear and concern there?

Yes, Andrew. I can see you.

The voice—the man's—slithered through Andy's head. Andy closed his eyes, tried to push it out, but it was still there. Deep. Resonating. Inviting.

I see you. I know you.

"My colleagues will remain where they are as long as you both cooperate," the man said.

You are one of us, aren't you?

"Where's Amos?" Andy said. Maybe if he addressed the man directly, he could force the voice from his head. But did he want to dispel it? There was something . . . comforting about it. Almost reassuring. Like the sound of a father's voice to a homesick child.

The man stepped to his left, then began to pace. "Amos. It's interesting that you bring him up." He stopped. "I know Amos, of course. Met him a few hours ago. Quite the interesting fellow. Feisty, though." He frowned. "Even uppity, I'd say. He wore out his welcome very quickly."

"Where is he?" Missy said.

"Oh, look, the blind girl isn't dumb as well. I was beginning to think maybe you weren't a threat after all."

Missy leaned her weight forward. "What did you do to Amos?"

"What makes you think I did something to him?"

Missy's eyes darted around the interior of the warehouse as if she heard something Andy couldn't. When she finally spoke, her voice was low, somber. "You killed him. Because of us."

The man smiled. "You're good." He lifted a hand and flicked his wrist. Behind him, one of the bikers broke from their formation and walked the length of the building to the south side. There he pulled a lever. The sound of metal disengaging was followed by the rattle of loose chains. Andy looked up in time to see a body fall from the metal rafters. It stopped about ten feet short of hitting the floor, bounced at the end of a chain, then swayed lazily.

It was the body of an older man, trimmed beard, short graying hair. His eyes had been gouged; dried blood covered his chin and neck. Amos.

Andy was glad Missy couldn't see the dangling Amos. Disgust and anger forced bile into his throat, and he had to swallow hard to push it back down.

"What is it?" Missy asked. Her eyes darted again.

"Amos," Andy said. He looked at the man standing across from him and, for an instant, wanted to rush him and tear him limb from limb. He could, too, but then he'd have to deal with the bikers, and he wasn't sure if even his strength could fight off all of them. He had Missy, though, and that had to give him the advantage.

Missy's mouth opened but no words came out. A tear ran from her eye, down her cheek, and followed her jawline.

Andy put his arm around her shoulders. "It'll be okay."

"It'll be okay?" the man said. "I hate to be the bearer of bad news, but it won't be okay. It certainly will not."

He drilled Andy with another evil stare. *I know who you are. I know who your father is. You're no different than him. Stop fighting who you are.*

Andy shut his eyes and pressed them closed. He knew he should push the voice from his head, but in some strange way, he didn't want to.

We will destroy you. And then we'll have our way with the girl. Or maybe we'll allow you to have your way with her first. You want that, don't you?

Did he know what Missy was capable of? He must. And yet he spoke with confidence. And how did he know the thoughts and desires Andy had wrestled?

"Andrew." The man stared at him again, grinning.

Your father wanted more for you than this.

"It's all lies, Andrew."

"What is?"

"What you've heard about your father."

He was a great man. A powerful man.

Andy never knew his father. He only knew what his mother had told him about the man. And what Clem had said.

He had a dream, your father. A dream for you. A hope. He wanted so much more for you than this.

As if she could sense the battle raging within Andy, Missy pressed herself closer to him and whispered, "Don't listen to him, Andy. You don't have to give in. You can make a choice."

There is no choice to make. You are who you are. Why choose anything different?

It was a plausible question. He was who he was. Half human, half demon. Wasn't that right? He couldn't change that. No matter what or who he wanted to be, fact was fact. There was a dark half to him. Why should he fight that? Wasn't it a losing battle? Eventually, his nature would surface. He'd seen flecks of it already, not just in the strength he possessed but also in the rage and hatred that often accompanied it, in the desires he felt and longed to satisfy. Those vile feelings came from within him, from somewhere deep in the moorings of his soul. They were who he really was. Could he change that?

Missy said again, "You can make a choice, Andy. You have a choice."

But did he? Could someone change his innate nature? Can a human decide to no longer be human just because he doesn't want to be human? Of course not. The thought was preposterous. So how could he decide to no longer be a demon just because he didn't want to be a demon?

Now you've got it. Now you're making sense.

Amos's body stopped swaying and hung still, the blank and empty eye sockets stared at the floor.

You are what you are. Who you are. No need to fight it any longer.

"Don't believe him," Missy said. "Please, Andy. I need you."
She did need him. He was her protector.

That's all you are to her. You mean nothing else. You never have. She harbors no feelings for you, no desire for you. And if she could see you as the freak that you are, she'd want nothing to do with you. Like the rest of them.

Andy now noticed that the bikers had inched closer. They no longer stood against the wall in formation. They had spread out around the room and were closing in, slowly tightening the noose around him and Missy.

Humans are so finicky. No loyalty in them. Given the opportunity, she'll betray you.

"Andy," Missy said, "you must choose who you want to be. No one can do that for you. There is a better way."

But was there?

The better way is to embrace your destiny.

"There is good in you," Missy said. "I've seen it. I feel it. Belle saw it too."

Belle. He'd let her die. She'd trusted him and he let her get shot. But she'd trusted him. She must have seen something trustworthy in him. She was a girl who had seen the world for what it was and found something in him, something worth trusting. Some good.

"If you won't choose for me," Missy said. "Choose for Belle."

Choose for yourself. This is what you were created for.

Andy looked at Missy, looked at the man. The difference between the two was so severe he didn't know how he'd missed it before. Not choose for her? He'd do anything for her.

He loosened his grip on Missy's shoulder and leveled his gaze on the man standing across from him. He was now very aware of the bikers just feet away on all sides.

He had a choice, and it was now clear to him.

Andy released his hold on Missy and sidestepped away from her. "I choose my true nature."

Chapter 36

The man smiled wide.

"Andy. No." Tears spilled from Missy's eyes and coursed down her cheeks. "Please. No." She reached for him, but he was already stepping toward the man and his wolf-like grin.

As Andy approached, the man extended his hand, palm up—a gesture of goodwill, an invitation to fellowship. He was welcoming a lost son home.

Andy took the man's hand and squeezed. Hard enough to turn his smile into a grimace. The man's eyes went wide. He sensed what was about to happen. Knew he'd been duped. Played.

In a move that was more catlike than anything an ordinary man could perform, Andy spun the man around so his arm twisted behind his back. With his other hand, Andy reached from behind the man and gripped his chin. Then in one quick motion, he twisted the man's head to the near breaking point of the neck's vertebrae.

The bikers stepped closer in unison. Their movements were coordinated and synchronized almost to perfection. Like the flocking behavior of birds.

"Stop," Andy shouted. "I'll break his neck. I will."

They knew he could and so did the man. The effort wouldn't even strain his muscles. In this position, it took about a thousand pounds of torque to break a neck, but that was not an obstacle too difficult to overcome.

The bikers stopped. All eyes were on Andy.

"What are you doing?" Missy asked.

"Do it," the man said. "Break it."

You want to. I can feel it. It's your nature to hate. Give in to it. You don't need to resist any longer.

Missy extended a hand toward Andy. Tears continued to stream down her cheeks. "Don't, Andy. This isn't the way."

"It's the only way and you know it," the man said.

I'll live in your head. In your heart. I will be one with you.

Andy cranked a little harder on the neck. The man grimaced and groaned. His body wanted to turn with the motion, but Andy braced it with his right arm.

"Do it!"

"No," Missy pleaded. "Don't. Andy, please don't do it."

Andy loosed the tension on the man's head. He knew that wouldn't be the end of it, that they weren't going to allow Missy and him to walk out of the warehouse and live out the rest of their lives in peace. But he didn't want it to go this way, not with him giving in to the hatred that had buried itself inside him. Yes, he may be part demon, regardless of what Clem had said, and yes, that dark half may be part of his nature, but he didn't have to give in to it. He didn't have to feed that black wolf. He could choose not to.

Andy kept easing off the man's head and neck until his hands were free and the man could step away from him.

The man rubbed his neck, then ran his hand over his hair, smoothing it against his head. "You're weak," he said to Andy. "I honestly hoped you'd do it." He then ran his eyes over the group of bikers and nodded.

Andy saw the nod for what it was—a signal—but he didn't react quickly enough. One of the bikers directly behind Missy leaped forward and placed a bag over her head just before tackling her to the floor. The other bikers simultaneously attacked Andy.

He tried to fight them off. He swung his arms, landing a few blows, shifted his weight, twisted and turned, but the force of fourteen burly men upon him was too much. He felt suffocated to the point that he was no longer able to move, let alone fight. Their strength individually was amazing; collectively, they overpowered him and pushed him to his knees, held him in a crucifix position.

The man crossed the room slowly and returned with a long sword. He stood before Andy and thumbed the blade. "Only one way to get rid of the two of you. I was hoping to wait until midnight to do this. It would have been so dramatic. So symbolic, don't you think?"

He then left Andy and walked over to where the biker held Missy. She too had been pulled to her knees with her arms held behind her back. The bag on her head was constructed of some kind of metallic fabric. She heaved for breath but said nothing, in fact, made no sound at all.

"No," Andy shouted. "Don't. Please, don't." Anger overcame him then, but it was not fueled by hatred. This was a righteous anger, fueled by love and loyalty and the desire to protect and nurture.

Andy strained against the men holding him. They struggled to stifle his movements and hold him in place.

The man stood before Missy, sword gripped with both hands. "You could have done this. It would have been so climactic."

"No!"

Outside the wind began to blow, the windows grew dark.

Missy seemed unfazed by all that was happening.

The man looked around nervously as the wind beat against the windows and the metal roof rattled.

Andy whipped his head back and forth in an attempt to generate some momentum and free himself. One of the bikers hit him in the head, over and over. The anger boiled over, and Andy could no longer contain it. He screamed and writhed.

The wind increased and howled like a pack of angry wolves clawing at the glass. At once, the windows shattered and the metal roof peeled away.

The man turned to the bikers and pointed his sword at Andy. He hollered above the roar of the wind. "Kill him!"

In unison, the bikers fell on Andy, punching, kicking, pummeling him on all sides.

Lightning flashed; thunder crashed and boomed, ripped through the sky and tore it open. Rain fell in huge droplets as the attack continued.

Andy had to do something. They'd kill him and then kill Missy if he didn't. He tried lifting himself from the floor, but the weight of the men on him was too much. He strained against them and again tried to move anything—an arm, a leg—but they had him pinned to the ground while they continued their barrage of blows.

Suddenly, pressure built in his abdomen and chest. He felt like he would vomit. Then the burning came, intense heat rising from his belly through his chest to his throat. His abdominal muscles contracted rhythmically like a dog preparing to heave. His diaphragm then joined in.

What happened next was not anything Andy had been prepared to handle. He turned his head as fire leapt from his mouth. In that moment, he lost control of everything. He felt the burn in his mouth and the heat of the fire against his flesh, but he could not contain it in any way. It was as if the fire had a will of its own.

Slowly, Andy faded from consciousness. He could hear men screaming and yelling, but it was distant as if he were miles away, listening to the sounds of hell transmitted over a phone line.

When he came to, he was lying on the concrete floor in the middle of the warehouse. His mouth was dry and tasted like sulfur. His throat burned. He quickly oriented himself. Above, the sky still roiled. The winds whipped. Thunder crashed. Lightning lit up the sky. Around him the charred bodies of fourteen men lay strewn across the floor like discarded fire logs.

The man was still there. And Missy. One of the bikers still held her with both arms behind her back. The man still held the sword. He lifted it above his head, ready to bring it down upon Missy.

"No!" Andy shouted. And as if his voice had triggered some meteorological phenomena, a jagged bolt of lightning descended through the open ceiling of the building and struck the sword. The electrical current traveled down the sword and through the man's body, lighting it up like a thousand-watt bulb.

The man dropped to the floor; the sword clattered on the concrete. The biker holding Missy suddenly looked confused, then went into convulsions. He released her and stumbled back, his body twitching and jerking. Finally, he fell to the floor and lay motionless.

Andy rushed to Missy and pulled the bag from her head. She reached out and touched his face. "Andy, what did you do?"

Chapter 37

The odor of burning flesh hung in the air like a cloud of dust, making it difficult to breathe.

Andy stood and helped Missy to her feet. "C'mon, we need to get out of here."

The storm had died and the sky had cleared. Sirens screamed in the distance. The storm had caught everyone off guard. Outside, people emerged from their homes and businesses, all gazing skyward. But the sky had turned clear again; stars dotted the now black backdrop. The warehouse appeared to be the only building hit by the rogue storm. Its windows were blown out, and the metal roof curled back like a dark wave in the moonlight.

As the sirens grew closer, Andy said, "We better get out of here. I don't feel like answering a bunch of questions when they find what's in the building. Think one of these motorcycles will do?"

Missy nodded. "Definitely."

Andy climbed on and Missy sat behind him. Andy had ridden plenty of dirt bikes and four-wheelers around the ranch in Kentucky, but he'd never tamed a Harley. He cranked up the engine and smiled at its deep, throaty growl. Yeah, definitely.

He backtracked his way to I-295 and took that north out of Portland. At Yarmouth, Andy exited the highway and found a secondary road that wound to the coastline and an overlook. There he parked the bike and got off. Missy did the same. The ocean sprawled before them, its green depths stretching all the way to the horizon where the line between water and sky was blurred. A gentle breeze, soaked with the aroma of salt, blew in off the water.

"You want to talk about what happened back there?" Missy finally said.

The breeze played with her hair as she tilted her head back and closed her eyes.

She knew what had happened, what Andy had done. There was no need to repeat the ordeal in detail to her.

Andy said, "What does it mean?"

"What?"

"The prophecy. Where does it lead?"

She was quiet for a moment. "I don't know. I guess we'll have to walk by faith, won't we?"

"Why us?"

She turned her face toward him and took his hand. "I don't know."

"We're no better than anyone else."

"We're just a couple of freaks."

They held hands for a few long beats. The ocean moved quietly, slowly. The water was remarkably calm.

Finally, Andy said, "It's not over, is it?"

Missy faced the water. "Not by a long shot. It's just beginning. There is so much more to do."

"They won't stop coming for us, will they?"

"They'll keep hunting us."

"And according to the prophecy, they'll kill us."

"I'm not looking forward to that."

"Me neither."

"Dying isn't cool."

"Nope."

"But even then," Missy said, "it won't be over."

"I'm not sure I can do this."

Again, Missy faced Andy and took both his hands now. "You

can. We both can. We must trust that the prophecy is truth. We must trust that our steps will be guided and that protection will come when it's needed. We must walk in faith. Every step. No matter where it takes us."

"You make it sound so easy."

"It won't be easy. But it'll be necessary."

"One step at a time. Will you be with me?"

"Every step of it." She put her back to his chest and wrapped his arms around her waist. "I'll never leave you if you never leave me."

"Deal."

She turned, keeping his arms around her waist until she faced him. She looked up at him with wide eyes, her lips slightly parted. She reached up and draped her arms around his neck. "Thank you for never giving up on me, for coming after me, for sticking with me."

Her closeness stirred deep emotions in Andy, and he almost began to cry. "Can you see me?"

She smiled. Her eyes bounced around his face. She lifted her right hand and placed it on his face. Lightly, with just her fingertips, she traced every line, every scar, every ridge and valley until she'd covered his whole face.

Andy's heart pounded in his chest; his breathing grew shallow and rapid.

Finally, Missy said, "I see all of you. And you're perfect. You're just the way you should be."

"I'm a freak."

"Then you're a freak that I love." She pulled his head down until their lips touched. Her kiss was gentle but passionate and pushed tears from Andy's eyes.

They held each other for a long time before Missy turned back around. The breeze blew her hair into Andy's face, and he drew in a long breath of her scent. "How will we know what to do next?"

She paused. "Amos was supposed to tell us."

"Amos isn't here."

"The prophecy says we eventually wind up in Jerusalem, so I guess we need to make some travel plans."

"You make it sound easy."

Missy put her hands over his. "Is that going to be your standard retort?"

"Maybe."

Chapter 38

Andy and Missy remained on the beach until the sun peeked above the watery horizon. Andy didn't sleep. He held Missy as the salty air and tumbling water kept him company. Thoughts swam through his mind, reviewing the events of the past several days. Never could he have imagined what would follow when he'd climbed into that drainage pipe. His life had taken so many turns; so much had transpired in such a short time. Enough to fill two lifetimes.

Strangely, he had a peace now, a certainty that all would be well. He knew the future held more turmoil and conflict, more rough waters, and many more forks in many more roads. But he also knew what the end held. He saw how it all would come together. And as long as Missy was by his side, he could cross any ocean.

Missy snuggled into him, and he kissed the top of her head, stroked her hair. He worried for her, wondered if she could endure to the end. Of course she could. She was remarkable and competent. She had a gift, and it consisted of more than the ability to breathe fire. She was chosen.

When the first rays of light split the darkness and reflected across the wide expanse of the Atlantic, Missy stirred and grunted. She opened her eyes and turned her face toward Andy. "Did you sleep at all?"

He kissed her cheek. "Not at all. I didn't want to miss a moment with you."

She sat upright and stretched her arms above her head. "Is the sun up?"

"Barely."

"I can feel its warmth."

The night had been chilly but not uncomfortable. Missy ran her hands through the gravelly sand. "What does the beach look like?"

"It's Maine, so it's not really much of a beach. It's rocky, large boulders here and there. Pine trees along the coastline. The water is calm this morning. The sunlight glistens off the tips of the waves."

"Like silver."

"Yes. Like silver."

"I went to the beach once as a kid. New Jersey. My mom took me early one morning so I could see the sunrise. I remember what it looked like."

Andy ran his fingers through her hair. "Can you smell the salt in the air?"

"Oh yes. I love it."

Movement caught the corner of Andy's eye. He turned quickly and found a man plodding along the shoreline, walking in the surf. He appeared to be elderly.

"Someone's coming," Andy said.

"Someone?"

He stood and helped Missy to her feet. "An old guy."

"Did he see us?"

"I think so. Yeah. He's walking toward us."

As the man approached, his features came into view. Andy recognized him immediately. "It's Clem."

Missy's eyes widened. "Clement? How?"

Clem waved and stepped around an outcropping of small boulders. When he got close enough, he said, "Good morning. You made it to Maine."

"Clement?" Missy said. "How are you here? I thought—"

Clem walked right up to Missy and put his hand on her cheek.

"I'm here, little one. That's all you need to be concerned with now."

He didn't have a mark on him, no wounds, no scars. The last time Andy saw Clem he was being attacked by a Doberman.

Clem sighed, clasped his hands in front of him, and smiled. "Are you ready?"

"For what?" Andy asked.

"The rest of your adventure. You didn't think it was over already, did you?"

"It's only beginning," Missy said.

"You're right. And you have so much ground to cover."

"I have some questions first," Andy said.

Clem lifted his eyebrows. "Questions? Why, of course you do."

Questions had been gnawing at Andy's mind since that first encounter with Colin. Questions that had gone unanswered for far too long. "Who were Colin and Trevor and the guy in the big rig? Were they . . . like me? Different?"

Clem's face grew serious. "Andy. Missy. There are others like me here to help you, but there are many others who will try to stop you. They didn't succeed this time, but that doesn't mean they'll stop. They won't. Not until . . . not until—"

"We're dead," Missy said. "I know. The prophecy."

"Colin and Trevor and the others," Clem said. "They weren't like you, Andy. They were pawns. Used and discarded by the enemy. They meant nothing to him."

"The enemy?" Missy's faced creased with concern.

"The man you met in the warehouse." Clem shrugged. "The enemy."

"The lightning got him," Andy said. "It killed him."

"Not by a long shot, son," Clem said. "He can't be killed. He'll be back at a later time, a more opportune time."

"What are we to do?" Andy asked. "Where are we to go?"

Clem reached out his hands and touched Missy and Andy. "You two are special. The world is about to turn very evil, and you alone will be the voices of truth. You are to be lights, and you will shine the brightest when the world is darkest. You will make a great difference."

"Are we to go to Jerusalem?" Missy asked.

"Yes. Your journeys will take you there. That is where you will encounter the enemy for the final time."

Missy nudged closer to Andy and shivered. "The prophecy."

"Let it guide you, little one," Clem said. "It is not something to fear. You both were meant for such a time as this. You were born for this purpose and this purpose alone."

"And what are you, Clem?" Andy asked. "An angel?"

Clem smiled and winked. "We all can be angels to someone, right? I'm a messenger, a servant. Nothing more. Nothing less. I've delivered my message and now my job is done." He took both their hands. His hands were soft and warm, his grip firm. "Now go in peace and walk with the eyes of faith."

Clem released his grip and let his arms fall to his sides. He smiled one last time and walked the way he had arrived. Andy and Missy watched him until he disappeared around a large boulder.

Andy put his arm around Missy and pulled her close. "Are you ready?"

"With you? Yes. Ready for anything."

Chapter 39

Transcript from NBC Nightly News, senior foreign political analyst Thomas Yearns reporting.

Tonight, in a stunning turn of events, the two religious terrorists who have plagued the Middle East for the past three and a half years have been killed. Facts are sketchy at best, but initial reports reveal a highly trained special forces unit of the United Arab/Aryan Brotherhood carried out a covert operation, which resulted in the death of both individuals.

The attack took place in Jerusalem on the corner of Rashba Street and Ramban Street near the Israeli Parliamentary Building at a little after nine o'clock local time.

Both bodies remain in the street, and bystanders have gathered to celebrate. Images of the scene have already been broadcast via satellite around the globe.

The man and woman, now reported to be Andrew Mayer and Melissa Abramov, both of Jewish descent but American citizens, began their reign of terror three and a half years ago with a series of gruesome murders. The pair is reportedly responsible for the deaths of over a hundred and sixty individuals over that period of time. They were also reportedly responsible for destructive weather patterns and phenomena around the world that claimed the lives of many more. Sources tell me the plot to capture or kill the duo has been in the planning stages for months, and many believe the attack came much too late.

Most believe this marks an important date not only for the Middle East but also for the world. While the instigators were successful in getting some to follow their teachings of hate and intolerance, most of the world's citizens viewed them as terrorists of the most heinous kind. There is already talk of establishing this day as a worldwide holiday.

As always, we will continue to keep you updated as these events unfold. But for now, rest well and know that the world is a safer place.

Reporting from Jerusalem, Thomas Yearns.

Chapter 40

Transcript from British News Corporation, Headline News, world news correspondent Jamie Butler reporting.

The world is in shock. Utter shock. The two international terrorists known by some as "The Witnesses" are alive. I repeat—it is midnight here in Jerusalem and they are alive.

Killed three and a half days ago by special forces in a highly covert and well-planned attack, the duo's bodies lay at the corner of Rashba and Ramban Streets in Jerusalem, located right behind me, untouched. So hated were they that their bodies were left to rot, many thinking they were not worthy of even an improper burial.

If you look just over my right shoulder, you can see the two standing almost motionless, faces turned skyward. They've been like that for nearly thirty minutes now. And, as you can see, a very hostile crowd has gathered around them. Fear is thick in this Jerusalem air. The terrorists are responsible for numerous deaths both in America and here in Israel, and the world celebrated when they were killed.

And now, inexplicably, they are alive.

The duo, recently identified as—

Oh, wait . . . what is happening? John, are you getting this?

For those viewing at home, John, our cameraman will attempt to capture what we are seeing in the sky above Jerusalem.

Are you getting it?

A massive storm front has just rolled in. The clouds . . . they're boiling, churning. I've never seen anything like this.

Bloody . . . the clouds are parting. They are parting, just rolling back like a wave.

John, John! The ground. Look what's happening. This is bloody unbelievable. The pair has lifted off the ground. Their feet are not on the ground. They are rising into the air. Ten meters, fifteen meters, twenty, thirty . . . Oh bloody sh—

[Loses transmission of video and audio]

John, did you get it? Did you get that?

The duo rose slowly into the air and then . . . just . . . I don't even know how to explain it . . . they were gone, like they grew bloody rocket boosters on the bottoms of their feet and shot straight up through the hole in the clouds.

I have never seen anything like this, John. I've never seen anything like this. I'm sweating, crying, shaking all over. This is bloody incredible. If I hadn't seen it with my own eyes, I would say anyone reporting this was bloody crazy. But I'm not crazy. Am

I? John, am I crazy? You saw it too, right? Did you get it?

The scene here is one of utter panic and chaos. The crowd on the street has mostly dispersed, most running from the scene. I . . . I can't believe what I just witnessed.

Uh, uh, reporting live from Jerusalem. Jamie, uh . . . this is bloody nuts. I don't even remember my own name.

71702601R00139

Made in the USA
Middletown, DE
27 April 2018